HUMBLE GREETINGS

THE FIRST HUMBLE GREETINGS NOVEL

ESSIE POWERS

LADY DAY

*T*he heat was almost impossible to bear. It rolled over in waves, kneading and smothering and then starting again. The car was like an oven baking her alive.

Bella Miles gripped the steering wheel tighter, immediately feeling her sweaty fingers losing their grip on the plasticky surface. She needed air — she needed *quiet* . . . she needed to get away . . . but then wasn't that just where she was headed?

With a glance at the sign by the side of the road — *Services ½ Mile* — she flipped the indicator and prepared to turn.

The services had clearly been designed some time back in the sixties. Decades before she had been born, in any case. It seemed as if nobody had so much as deigned to give the place a lick of paint in that time.

She eyed the gritty, concrete building.

On any other day she might've been brought into mind of a Second World War bunker but today it was an oasis. She parked up and headed into the toilets.

Only when she'd got the cubicle door shut — had somehow compartmentalised the car journey into another space of her mind — did she realise how hard her temples throbbed with her heart-beat. She pulled down the toilet seat — clean or seemingly so, *thank God* — and took deep, gulping breaths.

The throbbing at her temples was only getting worse.

She only realised she had drifted into a daze when she heard footsteps.

The hollow, *clack-clack-clack* of heels on tiles.

Acting on instinct, she snapped her head upward and stared at the back of the closed toilet door. She mentally traced the progress of the woman in high heels, in her mind imagining her treading over to the basin, inspecting herself in the mirror. Perhaps right now she was pulling out some mascara and twizzling the brush through her eyelashes.

Bella breathed in deeply.

And then — before she could help herself — she felt it coming.

She just about had the presence of mind to stumble to her feet, and to somehow flip the toilet seat upwards. Before she knew it, she was down on her knees, vomiting.

She breathed more deeply.

Felt as if someone was jabbing invisible needles into her brain.

That felt better.

She felt better.

Didn't she?

As she got to her feet, stumbling slightly, she reached for the toilet roll limply hanging from the dispenser. She ripped off a good few inches then made herself presentable. By the time she had flushed the toilet, she had clean forgotten there had been anyone else in there with her. Until she opened the cubicle door.

The first face she saw was her own, staring back at her in the mirror. She looked gaunt — worse even than she had looked that morning — pallid, hollowed-out eyes, dyed red hair stringy and frayed. She had had no thoughts of elegance when she had got dressed today. Since she'd had a good five- or six-hour drive ahead of her she had simply thrown on a grim grey tracksuit, a pair of plastic sandals.

Gradually, her focus shifted away from herself and onto the person staring at her.

And it *was* a 'person' . . . not a woman.

A *man*, actually.

He had to be in his late-forties, early-fifties. He wore high heels — an elegant ruby-red pair which Bella couldn't help but admire even despite the circumstances. He had on a short skirt which showed plenty of trim, well-shaven thigh. As her gaze swooped upwards, she noticed he had on a spotless white blouse, three buttons undone to expose a hairless chest. When she got to his face, she saw how the tips of his flaxen hair just brushed his shoulders. He was touching up his makeup.

When he spoke, there was a slight quiver in his voice. "I . . . I *am* sorry. I didn't think there was anybody . . . well, until I heard . . ." He jerked his head in the direction of the toilet cubicle. "Are you, ah, feeling all right? You're not . . ." he looked her up and down as if checking for a fledgling baby bump ". . . no, I don't imagine . . . the *heat* then . . . gets to all of us, I suppose."

Bella remained too shocked to move her lips. Her gut reaction had been to scream when she had seen his face — to tell him, in no uncertain terms, that men were prohibited by *law* from entering ladies' toilets. Now, though, having heard the man speak, having actually heard the tone of his gruff, sure, completely unfeminine voice and his skittish train of thought, she couldn't bring herself to see him as any sort of threat at all.

3

"Can I," the man continued, "uh, *may* I offer you something . . . a drink, perhaps?"

Still numb, she could only nod.

He hesitated a moment then — his pinched-lip expression shifting into a nervous smile — bowed his head and excused himself. He returned less than thirty seconds later with a bottle of water. Realising she was shaking, she took the bottle from him, managing to muster a slight smile. The bottle was freezing cold and perspiring. She unscrewed the cap and took a few gulps. When she felt her head cooling — that she was getting a better control of her senses — she straightened up then looked him in the eye. "Thanks."

He smiled lightly, inclining his head.

She took another few swigs from the bottle then turned her attention downwards, to the sink. With the man still standing over her, she splashed some tepid water on her face and around her mouth. Feeling as though she was getting back to normal — as 'normal' as she managed to get these days — she made for the exit.

"Uh, excuse me?"

Bella glanced back over her shoulder.

The man was still smiling gently. "I . . . do you really think that you're in a condition to drive?" He paused. "Where're you headed?"

Bella drew in a sharp breath. She had — of course — gone through countless mental exercises like these before; and wondered what she might do under circumstances when she found herself propositioned by some creep or other.

Not that this man seemed like a creep.

Quite the contrary.

Still, though, it wasn't exactly the Done Thing to indulge strange transvestites in service station toilets.

"Normonswold," Bella replied, already sure she would regret it.

" 'Normonswold' ? I could give you a lift if you like." Although Bella made no reaction at all, the man held up his hand, as if to resist any attempt she might make to reject his offer. "I live about ten minutes' drive away — just up the road, in Unthorpe." He smiled wider as if this would offer Bella further peace of mind . . . rather than do the exact opposite.

Bella took a step backwards and almost twisted her ankle, catching herself just in time on the hand drier. Could there have been anything in that water? The bottle *had* been sealed . . . She looked back at the man, absorbing his gaze, trying to work out just what he was thinking — just what his *true* intentions were.

"Listen," he said, holding his saucer-like hands down by his sides, "if you like you could call a taxi, but this time on a Sunday you'd be lucky if it turned up before nightfall. Who're you going to see?" He asked the question as if it was *obvious* that Bella didn't live in Normonswold — that Normonswold wasn't her *home* . . .

"My mother," Bella said. "I'm going to see my mother."

"And who's your mother?"

She hesitated. "Indigo Miles."

The man flashed his eyebrows then smiled. "Oh, *I* know Indigo. Puts on *cracking* cream teas." He blinked. "Well, why don't you call Indigo up and tell her that you'll be right on your way." He swung around a ruby-red handbag which matched his shoes, unzipped it and produced a purse from within. From the purse, he slipped out a piece of plastic and handed it over. His driving licence.

Bella took it from him and read off the name. "Kieran Eric Doores."

She glanced up.

The man was wincing, head cocked to one side. "Call me Dorothy — everybody else does." He stooped into her, his voice dropping to a whisper. "At least on my Lady Days."

Bella handed the driving licence back. "Here you go, uh, *Dorothy.*"

Beaming now, he squirrelled away his purse. "Call your mum up — tell her you're feeling a bit woozy. Dorothy will give you a lift home."

Bella felt conflicted. It seemed almost bad manners for her to make a show of being dubious of this man's claims. And yet it was also common sense. From the way he was smiling at her, she could only deduce that he was positively enthusiastic about her calling her mother to tell her what was going on. So — with another glance back at 'Dorothy' — she slipped out of the ladies' toilets and into the service station corridor.

"Mum? Hi."

On the other end of the phone, there was a telling pause. The *clink* of wine glasses. A series of throaty chuckles. Jostling, muttering voices gradually becoming more distant — quieter. Her mobile phone pressed hard against her ear, Bella's eyes settled on a peeling poster in front of her — somehow still clinging to the tiled wall despite the heat. It broadcast the not-unreasonable message: *Don't drink and drive*, with a gratuitous image of a man gripping the steering wheel and staring at the camera, his family all dead in their seats surrounding him. If it had been up to Bella, she might've gone with a more impacting headline — if not a more original one. Something like *Smashed!* or *Wrecked!* would have got the message across without the needling, smarmy, 'Don't drink and drive'.

On the other end of the phone, there was the percussive

whumpf of a door being swung shut. "Who is it?" her mother asked, in sing-song tones.

Bella broke away from the poster. "It's me, Mum. Bella?"

"Ah." Another pause. "Bella?"

For a second, Bella thought she might need to jog her mum's memory, but she seemed to get there in the end by her own accord.

"My darling daughter! Bella! How are you? What are you —?"

"Mum, I'm at Wrought Bar Services."

"What're you doing *there?*"

There was more than a hint of derision in her mother's voice, as if Bella had gone out of her way to plan a trip to Wrought Bar Services for just — you know — a day out.

"I had to stop for . . ." She scrabbled to put the situation into terms her mother would understand ". . . a coffee."

"And you're . . . uh . . ."

"Coming to visit — yes, just like I said on the phone last night . . . just like I said this morning when I rang?"

Bella pictured her mother screwing up her drunken gaze, sifting through the evidence, trying to reach some conclusion or another. Bella decided to break through her deliberations. "I'm ten, fifteen minutes away, and I've, well . . ." she glanced back at the Don't-drink-and-drive poster ". . . run into someone here — someone at the services."

"*Someone?*"

"It's, uh, someone called . . . Dorothy."

"*Dorothy!* Oh, how perfect! Wonderful! Bring her right over then, will you?"

Bella paused. She wasn't sure whether or not she should state something else. Since she'd gone to these lengths to confirm the validity of this man's identity claims, shouldn't she go just one step further — make absolutely sure? How could she be certain that they were even speaking about the same Dorothy?

"She's a . . . uh, he's a . . . uh . . ."

"An *absolute* scream! Just what this party's been crying out for!"

Bella's stomach squeezed upon hearing the word 'party'.

Her mother gave her no chance to raise her concerns, however.

"See you soon, darling!"

Her mother hung up.

Bella blinked herself back into action, noticing in short order that Dorothy had emerged from the ladies' toilets. She couldn't help observing how he glanced about sheepishly, as if knowing that he wasn't really supposed to be in there and yet unable to help himself all the same.

2

THE APPROACH

"So, what brings you back, then?"

It was the type of question which Bella always hoped she wouldn't be required to answer. There was something so intrinsically depressing about it. Such an inevitability too.

She turned away from the rapidly moving countryside outside the passenger window and smiled. "Oh, you know, just to visit."

Dorothy caught her eye briefly, gave the flicker of a smile, then turned his attention back to the road ahead.

Dorothy's car was something to behold. Although it wasn't much more than your bog-standard hatchback, Dorothy had put in more than a little work into making it his own. The air reeked of peaches and cream — owing to the teddy-bear shaped car freshener hanging from the rear-view mirror. All the seats were covered with a fuzzy, deep-purple material. In winter, Bella was certain that this was something of a Godsend — getting out of the ice and snow to wrap yourself up in a soft, cosy interior. On a day like today, though, the material had the unwelcome effect of bringing the sitter out in a full-body sweat.

The steering wheel — she observed — was also covered in the same deep-purple material. It was a wonder that Dorothy was even able to get a firm grip.

As Bella turned her mind back to Dorothy's question, she couldn't help wondering if she wasn't perfectly okay now — if she hadn't completely recovered from her bout of dizziness. All it had taken was a moment to stop and draw a deep breath. A sip of water. She longed for her car, which she had left precariously parked between a pair of campervans. That wasn't to say there was anything unpleasant about Dorothy's company — far from it; he had even succeeded in making her laugh out loud on several occasions — but it was more the fact that the reason she had come home — the *real* reason — was so she could have some time alone.

Some time to *think*.

And yet . . . well, she'd have time to think later — why shouldn't she open up to Dorothy in the meantime?

Bella glanced at Dorothy in profile, watching how he squeezed the steering wheel with great care, making minute adjustments. "I needed a change," Bella said. "Something different. You see, I was living in London, and it was a kind of . . . I dunno . . . it seemed like a waste of time."

Dorothy pouted but said nothing in response.

Bella took this as her cue to continue. "I'm a copy-writer. I write the phrases for adverts — you know, on TV, in magazines, on billboards?" she added, as they rumbled past a billboard showing off a Cultured Gentleman sipping at a tumbler of whisky.

In the trade, Cultured Gentleman was code for a grey-haired man, with grizzly stubble, dressed in a tuxedo. His most notable talent was in delighting women twenty years his junior whether that be on a yacht, in a casino or beachside.

"Pay well?"

The question blindsided Bella. "Uh, yeah, it does." She caught herself. "Well, it *did* . . . I actually resigned a couple of days ago. Decided I couldn't do it anymore. Decided —"

"To come home?"

Home.

Bella allowed that word to fill the void for another few seconds, and then recalled how she had grown to hate how she would so easily manipulate emotions with such simple, catch-all words like 'home' or 'family' or 'memory'. She recalled — oh-so-vividly — how she had once sat in on a focus group for one of the scripts she had written, watching on how a girl sitting on the front row of the viewing room had been moved to tears by a mother and father going to extreme lengths to rescue their child's lost teddy bear. When the focus group had filed out of the viewing room, she had noticed that the girl had arrived with only her grandfather. What Bella most recalled about the occasion was how the girl had kept her tears silent, hidden. If the girl's grandfather had noticed that his granddaughter was crying at all then it was well after the couple had slipped from Bella's sight.

Bella squeezed her eyes shut then opened them again. "I'm just visiting," she replied, sounding far more definite than she in actual fact felt.

"So what're you gonna do now?"

"I'm . . . not sure." Bella caught Dorothy's eye. "Well, I do have *some* ideas."

Dorothy said nothing.

"I was thinking of, uh, starting a business of my own." She eyed

Dorothy closely, as if she was worried that he might burst into fits of laughter at the very idea.

He remained straight-faced.

Buoyed, Bella went on, "I don't know why, but I've always loved greetings cards. It's something about them — sort of like letters, but not . . . kind of helping people to communicate with one another when they don't quite know how to . . . we can often write things down when it's impossible to say them out loud . . . and sometimes we can't even write them down at all . . . that's the bit that's interesting to me . . . I'd like to help people, rather than just flog them stuff?"

Dorothy parted his lips slightly, in a way which seemed to say — in no uncertain terms — *You are babbling nonstop shit.*

Bella was pleased to see Normonswold was the next turning.

Bella's family home — as it had always been — was located at the end of a winding dirt track which was flanked on either side by ash and oak trees. Although Bella had never been all that great when it had come to nature, she had once done a school project on local flora and fauna. Despite the class being encouraged to pick out a nearby field to undertake their studies, she had decided to shortcut that part, not getting any further than her own front gate. Then again, she didn't suppose that all the kids at school had had access to such expansive grounds.

As Dorothy rolled the car around the bend, the house itself finally came into view.

Ebbendevor.

To Bella, *Ebbendevor* had always seemed so much smaller than it should've been — than the lead-up along the dirt path implied it would be. That said, it was unblemished, painted a bright white (Bella's mother had it repainted every spring) so that it stood out amongst the otherwise green backdrop of trees and rolling hills. The house itself was asymmetrical with a tower sprouting up out of its mansard roof. So often, she had sat up in that tower, peering out through the window. From up there, it was possible to see the whole of the driveway, right to the gate. Whenever her family were expecting guests, she would sit up there, in the tower — usually with an adventure book featuring children and some anthropomorphic animal — and glance up often to see whether or not said guests had arrived. Later on, she had replaced the books with magazines, and then she no longer went up there just when expecting guests, but whenever she wanted to be alone.

Whenever she wanted to escape her mother and father's never-ending arguments.

As they got closer to the house — to *Ebbendevor* — Bella felt a strange pinching sensation in the pit of her gut. To begin with, she was certain the nausea had returned. That whatever afflicted her had come back. Just as soon as the sensation had come, however, it dissipated.

She knew what it had been.

That sensation she had so often derided — so often tossed about in meetings like a ball for playing with . . . for *selling* with . . . *Nostalgia*.

In a single stroke, all of those old feelings; all of those *memories* from being a young girl, drifted back over her mind's eye. And she couldn't help but give a slight smile. When she caught hold of her senses, glanced up, she realised Dorothy was frozen, halfway through undoing his seatbelt. "Are you, uh, okay?"

Bella flashed him a quick, unconvincing smile, undid her own seatbelt and reached for the door handle. "Fine," she replied, getting out quickly.

Again, even though Bella was a very long way from being the Outdoors Type, even she couldn't deny that fresh air, birdsong and springy grass underfoot had a kind of restorative effect. This was so far from the city.

Dorothy had already unloaded her luggage. She took it from him with another embarrassed smile. She hoped that she hadn't made a spectacle of herself on the way here. He *was* a total stranger after all.

"Pretty light," Dorothy said, nodding to her suitcase.

"Yeah, I only packed for a few days."

"Well, if you need anything in the meantime, I can lend it to you."

"Thanks," Bella said, unable to keep herself from smiling.

They had hardly got more than a couple of paces up the front steps before Bella overheard her mother's impossible-to-misplace *shriek* cutting through the air. Even now — even thirty years after birth — she still felt the same scuttle travel up her spine. It made all her muscles draw tight. Every hair in her body stand on end. How her father had put up with it for so long before becoming a Cultured Gentleman escaped Bella.

Then again, love was weird.

Even in the advertising world.

Bella was just about to knock on the front door when Dorothy reached out to stop her. She looked to him, saw he inclined his head to indicate the passage which went along the side of the house. She didn't think to question his judgement — she just followed.

3

THE PARTY

*S*ure enough, Bella hardly had a chance to take in the garden before she heard her mother rattle out another of her *shrieks*. This time — unfortunately — directed at her.

"Bell-*uh*! Bell-*uh*!"

Before Bella could gain steady footing, her mother bounded into her, throwing her arms about her chest, holding her in a rib-crushing grip. Bella somehow managed to utter the words, "*Hi . . . Mum*," before her mother was calling out to someone else across the garden.

Bella took her chance to shrug off her mother's death-grip and — simultaneously — to clock the state-of-play. There was a trio of other ladies, all of them — Bella registered immediately — in varying degrees of intoxication.

The swimming pool provided the backdrop, its placid, emerald-green waters lapping gently at the sides, unused by any of the invitees despite the warm weather. There *was* something oh-so-base about bathing in public, after all . . . especially for a *lady* well into her sixties (no matter how stringently said lady would argue that — *really* — she was still in her 'mid-to-late fifties').

The first lady Bella recognised was Adiema Smith, teacher at the horse-riding school just up the road. Given that she had the form and presence of a bull, Adiema was difficult to miss. Even more so since Adiema — Bella noted — was currently squatting up against some bushes at the far end of the garden, her dress hoiked up to expose her flanks. When their eyes met, quite apart from attempting to avert her gaze, Adiema began to wave frantically. She was so enthusiastic in her waving that Bella had no other option but to wave back before surreptitiously looking elsewhere. Back at another time — back before Bella had made the switch to real, functional bras — she had taken riding lessons from Adiema, as just about any other girl of a similar age in the village had. The Adiema Smith Riding School had been running for decades and decades (perhaps it'd really been centuries and Adiema was a — particularly well-fed — vampire). Bella found it difficult to envisage a day or circumstance under which the Adiema Smith Riding School might cease to operate, although it must surely come. The place had been an establishment throughout her youth and, now, her adulthood, too.

Another lady was sprawled out on one of the loungers arranged about the pool, a nearly drunk glass of gin and tonic beside her. The lady was waif-like, her long silver hair squeezed tight to the frame of her body. She wore sunglasses and could either have had her eyes wide open, staring up at the sky, or have just as easily been dozing the afternoon away.

As always — weather was no factor — she wore black from head to toe.

This was Florianette Rutherford, the owner and manager of the unnecessarily urbane Modern Styles, located just up the road in the village of Normonswold. Back before retirement — as much as she could have been said to have retired at all — Florianette had run one of the most exclusive boutiques in London, Nightwalker. Apparently tired of city life after some forty-plus years, she had come to Normonswold about five years ago and set up shop. People came from miles to Normonswold for no other purpose than to visit Modern Styles . . . Bella recalled — on more than one occasion — when she had come home for Christmas, or for some other purpose she had been unable to duck out of, she would always see at least one vaguely confused hip, young couple park up on the road and tentatively slip from their car to go and explore. These couples would always look over their shoulders as if someone they *knew* might spot them in the back-end-of-beyond.

Last of all, Bella took stock of the much younger lady sat by herself at a small garden table. She was slowly and purposefully turning over cards, pressing her fingertips firmly together before making her move. There was a nearly empty glass of white wine sitting in front of her. It took Bella several seconds to work out just who it was, and, even when she managed it, she couldn't help but believe that she was mistaken . . . and yet, here was the evidence held up before her eyes.

Harriet Tumblebeach.

It *actually* was.

To revisit — even briefly — her relationship with Harriet sent a tingle right down to the pit of Bella's gut. They had been best friends once . . . but that was a long time ago . . . before the *Incident* had occurred . . .

Then again, when Bella thought things through logically, she supposed it stood to reason, what with Adiema being Harriet's aunt. From what she had heard, Harriet was still living with her aunt. Harriet was wearing a neat, pink summer dress which complimented her sleek, blond hair and did wonders for her figure.

Realising that her mother was still yelling at someone — or *something* — Bella decided to see what the matter was. She didn't quite want to float the prospect — even mentally — of having to track down a decent retirement home nearby Normonswold in the near future so she could really do with her mother *not* talking to things that weren't there.

Thankfully, when Bella came up to her mother's shoulder, she saw she had good reason to be standing at the base of a tree and shouting up into the branches. There was a dog up there. A Jack Russell terrier if Bella wasn't mistaken. It was only a second or so later that it dawned on Bella that dogs didn't climb trees, at least not normally of their own volition. Curiosity driving her, she asked the question.

"Uh, what's he doing up there?"

Cheeks flushed from drink, her mother held her gaze on the dog. "Oh, *high spirits*, I suppose!"

This could mean any and all things.

And Bella had no intention of probing any further.

Her mother let loose an eardrum-splitting wolf whistle.

Temporarily deafened, Bella squinted up into the branches, hands cupped over her aching ears in case her mother saw fit to whistle again. The call had apparently had no effect at all on the dog up the tree. Only — perhaps — that his eyes had become even wider and the look of anxiety more pronounced on his canine face.

"Whose dog is he?" Bella asked.

"Robert's dog."

" 'Robert' ?"

"He's a . . . oh, you know," and her mother made a flurrying gesture with her hand which —to Bella's mind — carried no meaning at all.

Looking around and realising she was the only person dressed for climbing trees — dressed as she was in her tracksuit — Bella decided to take the initiative. She looked to her mother, who was already smiling widely, somehow in her drunken state managing to maintain the telepathic mother-daughter connection. In a small way, Bella had half hoped that her mother might attempt to talk her out of doing this . . . that she might warn her against the dangers of a broken arm, or leg, or *neck*. Her mother, though, had never shown all that much worry for Bella's personal safety, because — Bella liked to believe because the reverse was impossible to contemplate — she wanted Bella to *learn* from her mistakes; to become a better woman because of them. And so Bella decided to take this as another lesson designed to ease her out of girldom and into womanhood.

Who knew? In thirty years' time she too might be able to throw reckless garden parties for no particular reason at all.

As Bella surveyed the way-up, taking grip of a low-hanging, firm-feeling branch, her mother apparently decided this was the perfect time to fill her in on the current situation.

"Thought I'd just have some drinks, a few of the girls round, but things got a little out of hand." She gave a titter at this.

Feeling her grip slipping on the current branch, Bella shifted her weight and swung her foot around to the V-shaped opening in the tree trunk. She rested her foot there and glanced up at the dog, which was now wagging its tail and looking at her hopefully . . . or perhaps it was an expression of morbid amusement, waiting to see her end her life in one of the more imaginative ways.

Her mother went on, "Maybe I wanted to put the party on for

you, darling, though I have to admit I can't quite remember . . . you *did* say that you were going to get here earlier, didn't you, Bella?"

Now only a matter of inches away from the dog — if she was brave, she could reach out and grab the dog from where he was perched in the tree branches — Bella paused to take a gulp of breath and to implore the pores of her hands to stop sweating so profusely.

"I called you last night, Mum."

"Oh . . . oh, I see . . ."

If Bella hadn't known her mother so well or — more accurately — if she hadn't been so familiar with her mother's relationship with alcohol, she might have been genuinely worried about her mother's state of mind . . . as it was, though, this was just par for the course. As her father might've said before his desertion.

Bella looked the dog in the eye, seeing — from the way it was wagging its tail and backing up on its haunches — that it was considering jumping into her arms. She wanted to tell the dog to stay put for the time being, to just give her a moment to get a better —

The dog took a leap and Bella had no more than a split second to react.

Her first reaction was to throw her hands up to her face, as if the dog might be attempting to attack her. As the dog made contact, Bella somehow backed herself up against the tree trunk, managing to find her balance, and to cling onto the dog. She had to admit that — when it came to gymnastic acumen — it was one of her better moments. As she slipped and slid down from the tree with the dog in her arms, she was somewhat disappointed to find that her mother was looking in precisely the other direction. She supposed that the whole wanting-to-impress-your-parents thing never quite really let you out of its vice-like grip . . . even when you were into your thirties.

The dog gave a couple more squirms and then leaped free of Bella's arms.

Bella watched on as the dog sprinted away, its uneven strides sending it in one direction and then the other. She turned back to her mother. "I think I'm going to take a shower, Mum." She looked around the garden once again. "Seems like the party is winding down in any case."

Apparently having gone somewhere else mentally in that moment, her mother snapped back to the present. "Oh . . . that's fine, dear."

Bella knew it was foolish not to take a chance when she was given it. She gave her mother a weak, parting smile and then lunged her way across the garden, avoiding debris — overturned glasses, crumbs and scraps of whatever it was they had been eating. When she got back to the house, she realised she could hear a car engine rumbling its way up the drive. A small red convertible crunched around the bend and drew to a stop a few paces away. If this was another invitee then Bella was going to make short work of her — going to send her back home without further explanation. When the car came to a stop and the driver stepped out, though, she soon realised that it wasn't a 'her' at all.

It was a *him*.

. . . But not a *him* like Dorothy.

Oh, no . . . not a *him* like Dorothy at all.

He was broad-shouldered and had golden, slightly red-tinged, shoulder-length hair. Although Bella had never been the tallest, she felt as if he positively towered over her. She almost missed what he said when his honey-coloured eyes locked onto hers.

"You haven't seen my dog, have you?"

" 'Dog' ?"

And it was then that the Jack Russell burst out of nowhere and streaked into its owner's shins.

The man bent down and retrieved the dog, drawing him up into his arms, allowing its paws to rest on his shoulder. He cradled the dog as if it were a baby. As he did this, Bella couldn't help noticing how one of the dog's back legs peeled back a little of the man's t-shirt to reveal a hard six pack. When he spoke again, she admonished herself mentally and felt herself flushing at her momentary lapse of concentration.

"My aunt isn't here, is she?"

" 'Your aunt' ?"

"Aunt Flo."

It took Bella another few seconds to return to Earth. "Ah, Florianette?"

The man nodded.

"Yes, she's just . . ." but as Bella turned to lead the man around back, she realised that the black-clad figure — Florianette Rutherford — was already making her way towards them. Since she was still wearing sunglasses, it was impossible to tell in which direction she was looking . . . the effect was rather unnerving.

"Ready, Robert?" Florianette asked, brushing past Bella, the man holding his dog to his chest, and making for the car.

The man — Robert — gave Bella a parting, overly polite smile, and then opened the passenger-side door for his aunt to step inside. Once his aunt was settled, he placed his dog in the back seat. Robert had almost closed the driver's door by the time Bella's senses recovered. "Uh, nice to meet you . . . Robert," she said, immediately feeling like an idiot for having said anything at all.

He studied her steadily, his eyes never leaving hers. "Likewise,"

22

he replied, and then brought the driver's door shut, gunned the engine, and set off back up the driveway, disappearing from sight.

Bella took several moments to compose herself — sorting out her muddled mind — and then she turned around and went inside the house; steering her thoughts onto more realistic — if no less heavenly — matters:

A nice hot shower.

4

NIGHT SHIFT

$\mathcal{B}$y the time Bella had towelled off and got dressed in her pyjamas — the silk ones which her mother had left hanging in Bella's bedroom wardrobe apparently for such impulsive visits as this one — she felt cleansed and a little woozy. Better, though. There was no sign of that nausea which had gripped her earlier in the day. She was already downstairs by the time she realised that she heard voices. And she had already set foot through the kitchen doorway when she noted that the guests hadn't yet taken their leave . . . but, then again, why *would* they have done? Just because she was there?

All four faces glanced up at her as she stepped into the kitchen — her mother, Dorothy, Adiema and Harriet. Each of them had a steaming hot mug in front of them.

Bella hadn't had a chance to get her wits about her before her mother had got to her feet and skipped across to the stove. She didn't so much as give Bella a second glance before she commenced pouring out a steady trickle of hot chocolate into a mug. Grinning like a hyena, her mother gestured to the empty chair at the table and Bella took up a seat. She wrapped her hands about the mug and savoured the heat pulsating from within.

"So, Bella," Adiema said, her chubby, well-liquored cheeks aglow, "your mother tells us that you've come back to visit."

"That's what she told me," Dorothy said. "Story's consistent at least."

Bella looked to Harriet, expecting her to pitch in. When she met her gaze, though, Harriet swiftly looked away, and Bella was reminded — if she truly needed to be — just how the current state of their relationship was . . . which was to say there was no relationship. And which begged the question of just what Harriet was doing here, at Bella's mother's house.

When Bella looked up at her mother, she saw she was busy with her own hot chocolate. She supposed it was one of those situations where it was like-mother-like-daughter. Either of them could be seduced instantaneously by a good cup of hot chocolate.

"I . . . just wanted to get away," Bella managed to get out, and hoped that those assembled at the table wouldn't sense the slightly wobbly tone to her voice. "Have a break, you know?" When she surfaced from another delicious sip of hot chocolate, she saw — from the way they all stared at her — that she had failed her acting challenge.

"Beautiful flat," Adiema said, peeling back her index finger as she counted, "Smashing nightlife — or so I hear; and a cash-rich boyfriend with a terrific pair of buttocks, or so I've been led to believe."

Perhaps in other company — maybe if Bella's grandmother had still been alive — someone might've chided Adiema . . . but in this company there were only the grins of Adiema and her mother; two she-wolves. Dorothy, too, was beaming. Harriet was the only one who didn't look up from her mug of hot chocolate.

Adiema continued, "Please let me know when we reach the part where you need to 'have a break'."

Despite the situation — despite everything — Bella couldn't help but smile at Adiema's tone. There was something reassuring about Adiema, someone who had been part of Bella's life for as long as she could remember . . . even though Bella had never taken to horse riding like other girls in the village.

"I . . . we . . ." for some reason, Bella's focus settled on Harriet — perhaps it was the intuitive twitch which told her that she shouldn't really have been there. A lump formed in her throat. She swallowed it back. "Me and . . . *Daniel* broke up."

She made sure to speak the more formal version of his name — rather than the 'Danny' she and his friends always stuck to — hoping that it might demarcate a definite end.

Adiema clasped her hands to her mouth and stared at Bella with wide-eyed horror.

Dorothy's eyes nearly bulged from their sockets.

Bella's mother's lips parted, sealed shut, then parted again . . . but no sound came out.

Silence reigned until — with a *squeak* of chair legs against the kitchen floor — Harriet excused herself.

"Why didn't you say?" Bella's mother finally got out. "Over the phone?"

Bella breathed in deeply. Tried to get a grip on the myriad feelings flooding through her, seeming to want to burst through her solar plexus. "I . . . we broke up a while ago."

"A *while* ago?" her mother replied.

"A month or two ago, actually."

More silence.

Then Bella continued, "I quit my job."

Her mother seemed to have exhausted her stock of shocked reactions. All she could do was lightly shake her head.

In the end, it was Dorothy who spoke first. "You can do that greetings card business of yours now, then."

Bella felt a sudden rush of rage, quickly followed by intense embarrassment. She had to take several gulps of air before she reminded herself that she had confided in Dorothy on the ride over . . . that she had *opened up* to him . . . how could Dorothy — who she had just met — realise the implication of what she was planning?

Finally, her mother found her voice. "You quit your job?"

Bella looked to Adiema, then to Dorothy before she had the courage to look her mother in the eye. "That's right."

Although Bella spoke the words so easily, there was enormous gravity attached to them. Ever since Bella had turned eighteen there had been an understanding that — despite her family's wealth — she was to make her own way in the Big Bad World.

Even though Bella might've begrudged this at the time, she saw — over a decade later — that it had been For Her Own Good.

When she had left Normonswold and gone to London, she had taken whatever work she could get — waitressing mostly — and she had spent the evenings working on ideas . . . on 'visions' as she had termed them in those days.

Ever since she had been a girl — ever since she could remember, actually — Bella could recall having the most vivid dreams. She couldn't quite remember when it had started, but she had begun to note down the details of her dreams, almost as if they had been a film script. She continued the task — whenever she woke from a dream she remembered — even today.

Once her waitressing shift was over, Bella would go back to the draughty box she shared with another girl, spread out her dream log in front of her, and then — with another notepad — scratch and scribble away at the paper. What she was doing exactly, she was unsure. What she produced from the dreams weren't really stories . . . and neither were they poetry . . . to Bella, they were sorts of sculptures . . . abbreviated . . . open to interpretation. It had been a chance meeting — as so often these things happened — when she had run into someone who worked at *Raving Industries*, a PR firm. She had been serving one of the executives — Ongrida — coffee and had just happened to notice the story board sketches for a TV commercial which were within a transparent folder tucked beneath her arm. One thing had led to another — Bella could never remember *exactly* what she had said to Ongrida — and Bella had ended up interning at *Raving Industries* before being taken on as a junior copy-writer. To begin with it had seemed so right — that she had truly discovered her vocation — a way in which she could channel all those disconnected thoughts and images in a creative and meaningful way.

Now, though, she felt differently.

A long silence followed.

It appeared that nobody wanted to speak before Bella's mother had the chance.

And then Dorothy spoke. "Indigo," he said, referring to Bella's mother by name. "Perhaps we should make tracks." He met Adiema's eye across the table — Adiema prepared to rocket herself backwards and out of this awkward *family* situation.

Bella's mother spoke up. "No, don't go."

She said nothing more to clarify.

Seemingly more out of instinct than anything else, Adiema and Dorothy looked to Bella.

"I don't mind," Bella replied, somewhat truthfully. Given her mother's track record of giving advice in perilous situations, she couldn't see how Adiema or Dorothy could conceivably do much worse.

"These are certainly life-changing decisions," Bella's mother said. "And I'm sure that you've given them the required amount of thought. I suppose" — her mother looked away briefly, appeared to suppress a sigh, then turned her attention back to her — "I suppose that the question is more along the lines of what you're going to do next."

Bella hadn't the energy to repeat what Dorothy had already said. The idea seemed to have somehow taken on more concrete form just from being spoken out loud. Before this afternoon — before Dorothy had succeeded in prising the truth out — Bella hadn't confided in so much as a soul about her possible greetings card business . . .

When the latest silence had oppressed the kitchen sufficiently, Dorothy broke into an inappropriate grin and said — in a far-too-chirpy voice — "Coffee?"

5

MODERN STYLES

*R*obert came to with an enormous *thud*.

The first breath was the hardest.

He had to make a huge physical effort to drag it from his lungs.

And then — *little by little* — breathing became easier.

His whole body was slick with sweat.

The room felt like an oven.

He eased himself up on the heels of his hands, listening to the sound of silence which pressed in on him from all sides. That had always been the most unsettling quality about Normonswold whenever he came to visit his mother.

Peace and quiet.

Too bloody much peace and quiet.

Just how his mother managed to survive the sensation year round got the better of him. One thing was for certain, *he* would never get sick of City Life and end up in the back-end-of-beyond. Why would anyone want to seal themselves away in such an isolated place?

Slowly, Robert began to piece together the dream he had been having — it was the same one as always. He had been going at a flat-out run — *sprinting* — down a darkened corridor. There were long, rectangular windows on either side. A fierce breeze blowing the curtains through the gap. As he had run, he had found it more and more difficult to stay on track — to force his mind *not* to wander from his destination up ahead; not to stop still and stare out through one of the windows to see what was there.

In end, he had begun to slow.

Then he had looked.

And woken with a start.

Like always.

Robert threw off his duvet and got to his feet. He draped a nearby dressing gown around his bare shoulders then stalked over to the window and looked out onto the ever-silent, ever-*peaceful*, Normonswold High Street. Nothing to see. Just the winding, cracked asphalt lane. Trees hanging still in the pitch-black early morning.

He tried so hard to remember what he had seen through those windows, but still came up with nothing.

Finally, deciding that he was hardly going to successfully self-analyse himself at three o'clock in the morning when so many professionals had failed to do so, he quietly picked his way out of the bedroom and down to his mother's kitchen.

His dog — Woss — was asleep in his wicker basket in the corner of the kitchen. He twitched as he dreamed of chasing rabbits, or a face-off with a fox . . . perhaps some epic quest across marshland, birds fluttering out of hedgerows, chittering to themselves with panic.

Robert sat down at the table, thought about making himself a cup of coffee and leafing through his papers ahead of the meeting later on that day. Then he thought better of it. He would hardly be able to focus now that his mind was rushing . . . and it wasn't just his dream which had his mind flying along at a dizzying clip.

No, it was a girl.

The girl he had seen earlier that day.

He had no idea why she had . . . *affected* him so powerfully.

He normally had no problem with women who turned on their charms full blast — to be quite honest, he was *wary* to it . . . it was only the callowest apprentice who managed to get himself into a tangle with a businesswoman.

But this girl had not seemed like a businesswoman.

Not to Robert, at the very least.

Sure, she had stood proud. And she had been devastatingly beautiful. And yet, there was something else — *something else . . .*

Robert rested his forearms on the table and leaned forwards, gently putting more and more pressure across his shoulders and upper back. He felt his muscles tauten. Although he had only been to the gym the previous morning, it seemed almost like an eternity ago. He was honest with himself, he was nearly manic about maintaining a svelte, professional appearance. It was important that clients would not sense weakness of any sort — weakness in business was fatal . . . And then his mind began to race, to wonder whether, in the meeting to take place later on today, his client would instinctively just *know* that he had woken up in the early morning having bizarre, childish nightmares. And that said bizarre, childish nightmares had actually had some sort of an effect on him.

Robert breathed in deeply then raised himself back to his feet. He trod through the kitchen carefully. When he reached the hall, he flirted with the idea of going back upstairs, back to bed. But he couldn't resist. Whenever he came to Normonswold, he couldn't resist, at least one time, seeing the reason just *why* his mother had thrown away everything she had had in the big city for . . . well, whatever *this* was.

There was no small amount of secrecy surrounding the door with a secure lock.

Robert knew its secret, though. He punched in the digits on the keypad and then — when the locking mechanism whirred — he turned the handle.

Right away, that clean, somehow *sharp* scent of material over-whelmed him. There was something about clothes — *new clothes* — which reached him on an elemental level.

He allowed the door to swing almost shut on his heels, and then he went down the couple of steps to the shop floor.

Modern Styles was no Nightwalker — though no place was — but it still had his mother's fingerprints pressed all over it.

Just as had been the case with Nightwalker, there was abso-lutely nothing on the walls. Just stark, white paint. Then there were half a dozen mannequins. All of them wearing a different dress. Although his mother had always been tight-lipped whenever it came down to discussing her 'art', Robert couldn't help but remark to himself about the way in which she would always choose the emerald-greens, the ruby-reds, the amethyst-purples . . . it was difficult to reconcile completely, but if Robert had had to sum up his mother's taste in a single word then 'witchy' didn't seem a million miles away.

Robert examined a few of the designs, unable to stop himself from wondering just how that girl he had met today would look in them. What was *wrong* with him? What had *got into* him? He supposed that it was something like nostalgia — coming back to see his mother always brought such feelings on. When 'nostalgia' was floating about in the air, the conditions were perfect for bringing out all of those childhood memories; old loves, etcetera, etcetera . . . but even telling himself that, he knew this was different.

And — *Goddammit!* — he just couldn't get her out of his mind.

With a final pang of frustration, he glanced out through the store front windows. Seeing nothing but the deserted Normonswold High Street, he stormed back upstairs, to bed.

6

RETURNING PEACE

*B*ella sat opposite her mother in Old Couple's Café located down Disjointed Lane, just off Normonswold High Street. Earlier that morning, they had made the trip to Wrought Bar Services where her mother had dropped her off in the car park so that she could pick up her car and drive back to the house. Once Bella had parked up, her mother had suggested that they go out to get a cup of coffee. And there was really only one place in town which catered for this particular requirement.

The windows of Old Couple's Café steamed up as the grey skies beyond the glass let loose their torrent of rainwater. For some reason — in all the sepia-stained remembering of her youth — Bella had forgotten that it had ever rained in Normonswold . . . just one more piece of evidence, if it was ever needed, of just how powerful a weapon nostalgia was. Not that she would be using it any longer — any more than a retired industrial destruction operative would use a wrecking ball.

The décor of Old Couple's Café hadn't changed at all in the

past thirty years — Bella's lifetime. Although she would've been taking her life into her hands to have spoken the thought aloud, she supposed that there were specks of dust which had been hanging around this place since the turn of the century.

Old Couple's Café was adorned with a ramshackle collection of furniture — seemingly accumulated throughout the years from a variety of different places. The most striking feature about the place were the photographs nailed to the walls. Each and every one of them featured the titular 'couple' — Geoffrey and Diana Banks.

The original Happy Couple.

The photographs featured Geoff and Dee — as they liked to be known — in a variety of locales. There had been a time when Geoff and Dee had gone on a world tour, and this phase of their relationship was documented by a series of photographs with well-known landmarks (the Eifel Tower; Sydney Opera House; the Taj Mahal).

Back when she'd been at school, Bella had worked at Old Couple's Café on Saturdays. She could still recall how she'd felt before taking on the job — how she'd believed it would be something simple . . . something she could easily do on the side with her studies; something which wouldn't require any kind of mental effort on her part. Well, although she might've been right about the job not really requiring any kind of mental effort, there was no denying that the job had been exhausting. That there had been few days when Bella hadn't fallen into bed worn out after a long day's shift. It had been a good precursor — a decent induction — to the waitressing life which had initially awaited her in London.

Sitting opposite, Bella's mother was smiling from ear-to-ear, her hands wrapped about her mug, bringing it to her lips, sipping at her frothy coffee.

Bella glanced down at her own *black* coffee, considering its impossibly inky depths.

"It must be just wonderful to have a fresh start," her mother said.

Bella wasn't quite able to appreciate things in these terms . . . but she supposed that since they had an open dialogue going it would be a shame to waste it.

"It's . . . different," Bella replied.

To tell the truth, she hadn't got her head around the idea herself fully yet — the fact that she had simply gone and handed in her notice and then *run for the hills*.

"So," her mother continued, placing her mug down, "this greetings cards business of yours — tell me about it."

Bella felt her gut squeeze. She glanced about as if some distraction might jump up to save her. But there was no sign of Dorothy or Adiema . . . or even Harriet . . . She was just going to have to power on through.

Breathing in the sharp scent of coffee as it wafted through her nostrils, Bella commenced to explain. "My old job was wearing me out," she said, "I just wasn't capable of writing another piece of copy — writing something just to *sell*."

She paused and looked her mother in the eye, seeing if she was getting through. Her mother showed no sign of being beleaguered so Bella took her chances and went on.

"It's just so . . . *manipulative* . . . everything I was doing . . . I was only touching people in the most superficial of ways . . . there was no . . . *depth* to anything."

Her mother cocked her head slightly to one side. She pursed her lips.

Bella knew she was losing her.

And quickly.

Finally, her mother spoke up. "Is there something *wrong* with manipulating people? I mean, if you think about it, the whole world can be broken down into those terms. I need some food to eat, so I go to the supermarket . . . am I being manipulated because I happen to have watched an advert on TV about a certain supermarket and I decide to pay a visit to said supermarket?"

"Yes."

Her mother hunched her shoulders. "There you go, then . . . there's no avoiding it."

Bella wrestled with herself, and in the end — even to her own ears — she could only get out the lamest of responses. "It felt wrong to me."

They paid for the coffee, and — as always — Geoff and Dee made a fuss of Bella on the way out, telling her — as always — that it had been simply *ages* since they had seen her, and that they hoped to see her again soon. Bella just smiled and wondered whether she should ask for her old job back.

She walked along the road with her mother, headed home. As a matter of reflex, her mother popped out an umbrella, shielding the two of them from the slick drizzle which was falling. They walked their way past the lake in silence. Although Bella supposed there were countless daughters who revelled in the silences afforded them by their mothers, Bella had always found it a supremely depressing prospect. There was something black, all-consuming about it . . . as if they really had nothing else to say to one another. It was moments like these when Bella wished she had had a brother or sister — someone else to confide in. But she didn't.

Right now, to tell the truth, she didn't even have so much as a friend to count on.

Bella saw a sailing dinghy out on the lake — its blue-and-white striped sails fluttering against the grim skies. It was almost like a punch to the cheek when her mother finally raised her voice. To tell the truth, Bella had almost forgotten that she was there, walking beside her, keeping the rain off her with the umbrella.

"Are you planning on staying the night?"

Bella stared at the murky asphalt. Then she realised what she had already been so sure about . . . and she scolded herself for not having raised the matter yet. But there had been no time. There had been no *appropriate* moment.

The rain began to rattle off the umbrella now.

"Mum?"

"Hmm?"

"I was wondering if . . . wondering if I could come back home."

" 'Back home' ?"

"Yeah, you know, *to live?*"

Even as she heard the words come back to her, she knew just how stupid she sounded. She could still — *so clearly* — remember the day when she had walked out of the family home, declaring that she was going to 'do her own thing' . . . she had barely been eighteen, and she had been so proud. There had been not one doubt in her mind. She just *knew* that she would go out and prove herself right — that she would fulfil her dreams.

Now, though, she was unsure what her dream really was.

"Why, of course," her mother replied.

Bella studied her features.

She was unsmiling — staring off into the drizzle ahead.

When her mother realised she was watching, she finally gave Bella the flicker of a smile. And Bella realised that her mother wasn't at all *against* the idea — no it was more the case that she had been taken by surprise. As the two of them continued on their way, along the path, Bella noticed her mother's stride become lighter . . . that her smile became wider and wider. When they finally arrived back to the house — standing on the doorstep — her mother's mood seemed to have lifted so far that Bella had begun to worry. Right until her mother said, "We'll have to crack open the champagne."

And then — Bella had to admit — she started to believe she wasn't making an earth-shatteringly massive mistake after all.

7

MOVING BACK HOME

*O*ver the course of the next few days, Bella worked on getting herself established back in the family home. When she had driven back up on Monday, she had believed that it would be a difficult process for her to dismantle her life in London. On the contrary, it was only a case of boxing up everything she had acquired over the past ten years and lugging it out the door. As she prepared to step through the doorway one final time — taking in the shell of the flat she was leaving behind — she realised that homes were only *places* . . . and that they could take on whatever form their inhabitants required.

Bella had somehow got the idea through her mind that removing her possessions from the flat would be some kind of a Herculean task . . . not that it would be possible to accomplish with half a dozen medium-sized boxes and only her mother's help.

As they drove away, Bella couldn't help admitting that it was something of an anti-climax to watch the block of flats disappear in the rear-view mirror. When they hit the road back to

Normonswold, Bella could barely recall what her flat had looked like at all . . .

The weirdest part of the process was moving all the boxes into her old bedroom and realising that not everything was going to fit there. And so Bella turned her mind to establishing the essentials — to unpacking a decent portion of her wardrobe; all she would need, on first blush, for the coming days and weeks. With her mother's help, she lugged the boxes up into the attic and left them in a corner.

Her mother seemed to appreciate the magnitude of what Moving Back Home really meant, and she was content to stand on the side-lines, not really saying much of anything — arms folded, a half-smile settled on her lips . . .

A strange thing happened once Bella had established herself back in her old bedroom. She had the sudden urge to *get away* — to *go* somewhere else. She left without telling her mother, emerging into the sunny daylight outside.

As she walked along the driveway, headed into Normonswold, she noticed how the leaves were beginning to turn with the autumn — how they were gradually turning gold and silver about the edges. When she got to the end of the drive, she just kept on going. And before she knew it, she was walking through the village itself, taking stock of all the shopfronts. It was only when she reached Modern Styles that something stopped her otherwise casual stroll. There was a sign in the window, hanging just behind the glass. There was no ambiguity to what it said, and yet it took Bella several moments to properly process its message:

Closing down — all stock must go.

She looked from side to side, as if she might find herself being

the centre of some kind of elaborate — not-too-funny — wind-up
. . .

There was no one there, though.

She was all alone.

It was then that she noticed someone peering out of the window from the floor above.

She tilted her head back to look — with a flutter of her heart seeing that it was the man she had briefly met the day before. He hadn't seen her yet. He was merely standing in the room, in profile. He had a phone pressed up against his ear, and he was jabbering away animatedly.

Bella couldn't lie to herself, she had seen more amateur sleuth TV shows than was probably good for her, and she jumped to her conclusion almost immediately:

Murder.

A jealous son returning home.

Looking to assume his mother's property before time.

Acting without thinking things through, she rushed past the closed storefront and hammered her fist against the front door of the cottage. The rap of her knuckles echoed within. She only stopped when she heard the brushing of socks against hallway carpet.

When there were a few muffled barks.

Bella breathed in short sharp breaths, looking around for a blunt object, ready to face up to the man — Robert? — who would surely soon darken the doorway, looking to brush things over . . . to get Bella herself out of the picture . . . and that was when Bella began to fear for her own safety; when she started to worry that if what she suspected was truly correct then she had succeeded only in throwing herself in harm's way. And what would that achieve?

When the door finally did open, however, it wasn't Robert who stood there at all.

It was Florianette.

Bella had hardly a moment to absorb the sight before a guided missile zipped out from between Florianette's legs. As something furry and warm brushed her shins, the conclusion struck Bella that this was the dog she had saved from the tree back at her mother's house . . . back at *her* house. She took stock of the lolling tongue and the large, loving eyes. Because there seemed nothing else for it, she crouched down and gave the dog a few good scratches behind the ears. His eyelids fluttered closed and he tilted his head upwards; tongue wagging about his jaw in pleasure. Bella turned her attention back onto Florianette, and realised — almost immediately — that something was terribly wrong.

Florianette looked skinny . . . well, she had *always* been skinny . . . but now she looked positively *gaunt*. To begin with, Florianette did not seem to recognise her and she found herself saying, "It's me — Bella Miles? From down the road?"

There was a spark at the back of Florianette's eye, or perhaps it was nothing more than a twitch. It was then that Bella heard more footsteps.

"Who is it, Mum? Who's at the door?"

Florianette and Bella simultaneously shifted their focus to take in the person approaching. It was Robert — the man Bella had met in the driveway . . . the owner of the dog Bella had saved from the tree in her mother's garden.

"Woss, come! Stop bothering this lady."

The dog immediately ceased pressing his furry body up against his saviour's leg and trotted to his owner's side where he sulked obediently.

Robert fixed Bella with a grim smile and reached for the doorknob. "I'm sorry," he said. "This isn't a good time. Apologies." And — with that — he made to shut Bella out.

It was then that Florianette seized some degree of strength. She held her arm up, blocking her son from shutting the door. Although Robert appeared reluctant to allow this protest, he did nothing to force the matter. This *was* his own mother, after all. Finally, Florianette addressed Bella in a frail, almost impossible-to-hear voice.

"It's not good news, Bella — not good news at all."

Bella continued to stare back into Florianette's eyes.

And then Florianette blinked.

The spell was broken.

Noting the tension in the air had dissipated, Robert gave Bella another smile, and then reached out and closed the door. Through the tiny, final slit as the door finally closed, Bella caught Robert's eye, and something passed between them. It was something almost mournful, and a connection definitely more meaningful that one which had been forged between total strangers. Bella felt a tightness squeeze her gut.

And then she was alone again.

On the doorstep.

8

HUMBLE GREETINGS

*T*he news of Modern Styles's closure — and of Florianette's illness, which meant she had to move closer to the city— swept through Normonswold as it only could in a small town. Somehow Bella felt guilty for having imposed herself on the situation — for having knocked on the door of Florianette's cottage that particular day. And yet, at the same time, she realised that she had been faultless. It had just been an impulse . . . albeit a perhaps slightly impolite one . . . she supposed she could've phoned ahead, and yet people in Normonswold prided themselves on their neighbourly attitudes — how nobody needed to lock their doors at night, and how the kettle was always at the ready for whenever anybody wished to pop in for a cup of tea.

Bella spent the days at her mother's kitchen table with page after page of blank paper. She would scribble anything and everything which came to mind in relation to her business idea. She was amazed at how previously unrelated and unnoticed connections knotted themselves together so neatly and formed coherent ideas.

She soon realised that what sat at the centre of her business was communication — that was her goal; she wanted to help people to communicate better . . . or — maybe more accurately — to communicate *at all.*

She had only to think of her own life. Of all the relationships she had personal experience of where people couldn't say *anything* to one another; how they could only speak about things in *superficial* terms . . . the clothes they wore, the people they knew, the TV programmes they watched . . . what good was that? When she really got down to it, she realised how much time in life was wasted.

How could she reduce that waste?

And that was when the name struck her — seemingly out of the blue.

It was a *greetings* card company . . . and the message would be humble . . .

Humble Greetings

It said all she wanted to say.

And — on one blank piece of paper — she wrote the name in the centre.

Then she put the kettle on.

As the days went by, Bella was surprised at how many calls and emails she was required to field — people who she had known back in the city who wanted to hire her for this or that particular assignment. To begin with, when she received the requests, she would treat them tentatively. There was still some basic survival mechanism functioning at the back of her brain — some little voice gently nudging her, chiding her not to burn any bridges . . .

not to lose chances for work further along the line . . . to *keep her options open* . . . and yet something from within her — *something so loud* — told her that she was only fooling herself to lead these people on. Her mind had already been made up.

Humble Greetings was her future.

It was mid-morning when the house phone rang. Since her mother was out at the supermarket — a good half an hour's drive away — Bella picked up and answered.

"Indy?"

Bella was surprised at the gruff voice on the other end of the line. She had the urge to leap in and act the protective daughter with this unsolicited male caller.

"Who is this?"

A pause on the other end of the line. "It's Kieran."

Bella turned her attention out of the window, to the storm clouds brewing on the horizon. "And what do you want with my mother?"

Another pause. "Bella?"

Now Bella felt truly freaked out . . .

"It's Kieran — *Dorothy*, you know? I gave you a lift a few weeks ago. I didn't think you'd still be, well . . . I suppose you're actually going to do it?"

Bella's pulse hammered at her temples. And then she recalled how she had confided in 'Kieran' while in his Dorothy persona. She shifted her focus back onto the phone — back onto the voice on the other end of the line.

"Yeah," she replied. "I'm going to do it."

"Oh, that's good." Kieran/Dorothy's reply made it seem that it was such a simple matter — such a *trivial* matter . . . when, in reality, it was anything but . . . "I have some news, Bella."

"Okay?"

"I mean, I was hoping to speak with your mum about it first, but I don't suppose she'll mind hearing it from you, either way."

"Go on."

"It's Florianette — her condition is terminal."

It felt as if someone had struck Bella with an invisible sledge-hammer to the solar plexus. To begin with her chest was impossibly tight . . . she couldn't drag so much as a gasp of air from her lungs. "I . . . I'm sorry."

"I . . . I'll see you soon," Kieran/Dorothy said with a sniff and then hung up.

Bella sat at the kitchen table for the longest time, willing her ears to hear the sound of her mother's car crunching its way up the driveway, back to the house, returning from her shopping trip. So that Bella could get this enormous weight off her chest.

She had known that the situation was serious. And — what was more — she had taken a few guesses at the possible outcome. She had known that the situation *had* to be serious for Florianette to have decided to shut down Modern Styles. And yet to have it spelled out to her in no uncertain terms really took the wind out of her.

Terminal.

The end.

Florianette's funeral took place at Normonswold Church. Somehow Bella had expected the funeral to take place elsewhere; for Florianette to be returned and laid to rest in London, where she had spent the vast majority of her life . . . where she had set the sure foundations of her clothing empire. The service was well attended — any standing room at the back of the church was fully taken advantage of by the immaculately well-dressed mourners. Sitting beside her mother in the second pew from the front, Bella craned her neck to absorb the faces, to see all of those who had come to pay their last respects. She played a morbid game with herself, guessing at which ones had been life-long friends, and which might've been former lovers. She could read just about anything she wanted from the stony expressions — each and every stranger was a blank page just waiting for her to fill in the details.

The wake took place at Florianette's cottage. Like the other cottages throughout Normonswold village, it had a name: Molinaar's Cottage. Bella supposed that the house must date from sometime in the sixteenth century, back when it had belong to some noble village man. As she made her way up the path to the front door, she couldn't help but notice how tastefully the storefront had been adapted into the façade of the building . . .

She noticed today that — as they had been in the days following Florianette's death — the Persian blinds had been drawn down to hide the mannequins within. She wondered if Robert had gone through the process of undressing the mannequins yet, or if he had left them dressed in whatever his mother had last put on them as a kind of dedication.

The wake was just as well attended as the funeral. Despite the chilly weather, the mourners were forced out into the garden so that there was space for everyone and their paper plate of buffet food.

When Bella came upon Robert, their eyes crossed briefly, and he gave the gentlest of nods before moving onto the next person in line. Bella found her gaze drifting downwards to Robert's dog, sitting obediently at his calf, his sombre expression almost comically mimicking his master's.

Bella had often had the sense that Florianette had something of the proverbial Wild Child about her, and so she expected — at any moment during the wake — that someone might scream something out loud and a fight, or a dance, or *something* might commence.

The fact that nothing at all happened felt like an anti-climax.

When the time came — sometime just after eight in the evening — the wake simply dispersed. Bella made an effort to seek out Robert and his dog, but she was not successful. She had no idea where the two of them had got to, but the message was clear.

They were no longer available.

As she walked back with her mother to their family home, she had no idea what to say. So she said nothing at all. It was only when they got back into the kitchen, and Bella had put the kettle on, that her mother spoke.

"Bella? When I die, I don't want things to be so . . ."

Bella sifted through the mugs on the rack, pausing to examine one of them for much longer than necessary.

"I don't want things to be so . . . *stilted.*"

Unable to really penetrate what her mother was getting at — a funeral was a funeral — Bella decided she was better off just pouring the boiling water and making the two cups of tea. Once she'd splashed in the milk and given it a quick whisk with a teaspoon, she handed over her mother's mug and took a seat opposite at the kitchen table. Bella supped her tea in silence, doing whatever was necessary *not* to look her mother in the eye.

She thought her mother might start speaking about the funeral she *did* want, but — thankfully — she appeared to be through with discussion for the time being.

At around half past nine, the two of them went their separate ways, to bed.

9

WELL-MADE PLANS

*T*ime went by as much as it had done before Florianette's death and subsequent funeral. Bella filled her days with planning for Humble Greetings . . . how she should go about making her entrance into the business.

One of the largest stumbling blocks she had come across had been the simple and insurmountable fact that she was a lousy artist. When Bella had first begun thinking of starting her own greetings card company, she had somehow got into her head that she would be able to scribble together some minimalist doodles to accompany her crisp, on-point copy.

But it wasn't as easy as it had looked.

She had gone through the process of pulling several how-to-draw guides off the internet and then taken to practising on a variety of scraps of paper — just trying to get *something* useable out of what she doodled. But it was no good. It wasn't so much a case of not being able to draw, it was more a case of not having any idea at all of what it even was that she was *going* for! In the end — as

any girl should do given the appropriate set of circumstances —
she decided to consult her mother for advice. As always, as she
always supposed it was for other girls, her mother's advice was
right . . . if not what she wanted to hear then at least the Truth.

"Hire someone to do it," her mother said.

The two of them were standing outside the house, where her
mother was busying herself watering the flowers, dressed in a
cornflower-blue summer dress which was *surely* completely inappropriate for the cold snap they were currently going through.

" 'Hire' someone?"

Her mother continued to water the current batch of flowers —
exactly what species they were Bella had little idea. "Well, you
wouldn't need to take them in on a salary. Nothing like that. At
least not at first. You could try them out, work-for-hire,
you know?"

Bella *did* know, and yet why hadn't she given the matter any
thought whatsoever? After she'd done some thinking about the
issue on her own, she decided that it was more the case that she
saw Humble as an extension of herself. It was going to reflect her
innermost, truest expression. And to let someone into that vision .
. . well, wouldn't it water down what she had intended all along?

All the same, Bella knew — in real terms — that she simply
couldn't go forward with Humble with herself as the illustrator. It
was just as her mother had said.

She needed help.

And so she put out feelers online. She was wary of tapping the
veins of her former contacts, still unwilling to share just *why* she
had given up such a lucrative line of work for . . . well, whatever it
was she was doing right now.

Through various sites, she got in touch with designers and
illustrators, and she gave them a brief, asking them to put together

a series of samples to fit the pieces of copy she had put together for the first line of cards for Humble Greetings.

When Bella got the first responses, she felt close to despondent. They came from experienced designers — experienced designers who Bella had *happily* not happened to bump into during her time in London — and yet what they had produced for her were nothing but slick, polished illustrations which would looked wonderful on Tube adverts, or on the side of a bus, or perhaps even on a fifty-foot banner . . . but for the greetings cards, as Bella had envisioned them, they were completely wrong.

It was at the end of what was turning out to be a long week — what with her mother suffering from a cold and bedridden — that Bella finally had some reason for hope.

One of the illustrators sent her samples which looked useable.

Oh, sure, Bella would need to work closely with her to begin with, to make sure that they were working off the same page, but there was *hope*.

Working quickly, Bella dashed off an email, inviting the artist to come and visit sometime soon, and then she went to go and take her mother a bowl of leek and potato soup served with a hot, well-buttered roll.

A day or so later, as Bella was leaving her mother to her bed, after bringing her some tea, her mother spoke up. Bella saw her mother was pointing at something on the chair beside her bed. To begin with, Bella thought that her mother was maybe suffering from some kind of fever-induced delusions, but she soon realised there was a newspaper on the chair. It had been well thumbed and left squashed open on one of the back pages.

"Want me to throw this out, Mum?"

"No," her mother replied, voice still weak — *sickly*. "Take a look. Tell me what you think."

Bella held the newspaper up to the light, trying to see what it was that her mother wanted to draw her attention to. Wherever a newspaper was concerned, it was usually a matter of some politician doing something foolish, or else a celebrity who had committed some public sin. It was all a lead-up for her mother to shake her head, look dour, and mutter the eternal words, "Such an embarrassment."

This time, however, Bella realised that she wasn't looking at the celebrity scandal pages at all. In fact, she realised she was on the property section.

Bella frowned at this.

There was no doubt her mother was suffering from feverish delusions now . . . if there was one thing her mother was adamant about, it was that she was never going to leave this house so long as she was living — Bella couldn't count the times her mother had iterated that she would be 'dragged from Ebbendevor, kicking and screaming' or never at all. On more than a few occasions, her mother had subtly gestured to preferred, potential burial plots. Bella never had the heart to tell her mother that most likely when she did float on to whatever — *whatever* there was beyond —the house was probably going to be sold, if only to take care of the arrears which would've built up following the lavish funeral her mother had laid out oh-so-vividly in her will, despite her claims that she didn't want anything as 'dramatic' as Florianette's send-off . . .

Bella examined the newspaper a little more closely — and now she saw what her mother had wanted to draw her attention to. It was Florianette's home, Molinaar's Cottage, which was up for sale.

"Oh," Bella said, and then, blinking a few times, as if to bring the page of the newspaper a little clearer, "I see." She glanced up at her mother, worried that she might've become tearful all of a sudden, if this ad had served as some kind of a reminder of her recently departed friend.

Her mother, however, was straight-faced, emotionless. Maybe her cold had left her drained, without the energy to emote. "So? What do you think?"

Bella folded the newspaper over and held it down at her thigh. "Well, it's a shame, I suppose."

"A 'shame' ?"

Bella hesitated, wondering if her mother expected her to explain in greater detail just what this 'shame' exactly entailed. "Yes, you know, Modern Styles was very well thought of . . . it had an, uh, national . . . *international* reputation."

Her mother rolled her eyes and held up her hand. "Yes, yes, but don't you *see*?"

"See *what*?"

"The opportunity."

"*What* opportunity?"

Bella was beginning to get frustrated now. As always happened when she was losing her patience with someone, she felt a heat flush her face, and a tremble enter her voice.

"You can buy it — make it your headquarters. Make it Humble Greetings's headquarters."

Bella had no idea what to say to the suggestion. It sounded so . . . *off* . . .

"Listen, dear," her mother said, propping herself up in bed with a pillow. "I know you were planning to start things off from here, from the house, and that you were going to work towards finding your own place, working out just *where* to locate the business —"

56

Bella tried to interrupt but her mother held up her hand once more.

"But this would be perfect — don't you see?"

"No, I don't . . ."

Her mother clucked her tongue. "For Florianette, Modern Styles was the love affair of her life. It was the most important thing for her . . . something of her own."

"But what about Nightwalker, you know, that place she had in London for all those years?"

Her mother shook her head. "That wasn't her real passion — she never *really* put herself fully into Nightwalker. Not really."

Bella held her silence.

"Modern Styles was where she truly expressed herself, away from all others. Pure. Undisturbed. *Unique*."

Bella felt as if she was plunging through the floor, as if invisible hands were pressing down on her shoulders as if to drown her in a bottomless sea. And then, through her dry throat, she spoke the first thing which came to mind. "I . . . don't have the money, Mum."

As with everything else in the conversation thus far, her mother dismissed it with a simple wave of her hand, like some all-powerful enchantress. "It doesn't matter — we'll work something out."

SETTLING IN AGAIN

*B*ella felt as though Molinaar's Cottage was a badly fitting pair of trousers. As if — whenever she tried to pull the waistline tight — they would simply sag and fall to the ground. It was strange to think of how few possessions she had acquired over the years . . . that she barely had enough *things* to fill a bedroom, let alone a sitting room, or a dining room, a *kitchen* . . . and she didn't dare think about the shop floor — what had once been Modern Styles, and what was now going to be Humble Greetings . . .

With a scarf holding her hair tight to her scalp, Bella worked to get rid of the last box. She tossed it into a corner of the entrance hall, ready to be collected the next day. When the box made contact with the wall, someone rapped their knuckles against the front door. It seemed to happen at the exact same moment.

A shudder ran down Bella's spine.

She had never quite got over the idea of ghosts as a young girl, and she was quite successful at spooking herself given the chance.

Was this the reward she was going to get for having committed heresy — or whatever the word was for treading where the recently deceased's dreams lay?

"Come in?"

Bella watched on as the front door gently opened and through the gap emerged a mousy-looking woman of about thirty. She had strawberry-blonde hair and wore a men's great coat which was comically too large for her. To begin with, Bella felt as confused as the girl looked. And then the penny dropped.

Breaking into a grin, Bella trod towards the girl. "Cassandra?"

The girl's round, wide eyes drank Bella in. "Yes, that's right."

Bella realised the girl wore a messenger satchel swinging against her lower back. Bella fixed her gaze upon it as if it contained jewels of inconceivable value.

Then again, perhaps it did . . .

In what Bella was calling a kitchen — there was an electric kettle and a pair of mugs at least — the two of them stood and sipped at hot tea. There were no chairs or a table as yet. They would hopefully arrive in the next week or so.

As they drank their tea, Bella analysed the girl, noting how she had a certain skittish nature about her. She wondered if it was just because she had come here — to an unfamiliar place, or whether this was some fixed aspect of her personality. She tentatively decided to put it down to a lack of confidence. Given the girl's age, she supposed that she felt something of an imposter. This would be her first job. More than anything, Bella wanted to reassure the girl that if her work was as good as the samples she had sent her then she had nothing to worry about . . . the girl had no reason to think of herself as an 'imposter', in any case.

The girl set her empty mug down on the kitchen counter. She met Bella's eye for the briefest moment and gave her the merest hint of a smile. "Would you like to see my sketches now?"

"Okay."

The girl glanced about, as if a table might've materialised in the time they had been standing there, but there were — of course — only the mugs and the kettle for furniture.

She snapped open her messenger satchel and slipped out a pair of sketch books which she lay down on the kitchen counter. She looked to Bella another time — apparently seeking approval — and then peeled open the cover of the first sketch book.

Bella stood looking over the girl's shoulder, as if this might give her the best way into the girl's perspective — so that Bella might see what it was that the girl herself saw.

As the girl turned the pages, Bella felt her jaw slipping closer and closer to the ground. There was something eerie about the sight — about how, with the turn of each page, she saw her dreams coming to life. Her eyes fixed on the pages as the girl turned them, and the only impression she could identify — aside from the shock that she had found some sort of a *soul* mate in this girl — was the quantity of work this girl had produced. The samples she had sent Bella hadn't been the only sketches she had done in hope of landing this job.

No, it appeared that the girl had committed *hundreds* of sketches to paper in search of the right style.

When the girl had reached the end of the first sketch book, Bella had seen enough. Because her throat felt tight, and it seemed as if it would be impossible to attempt to speak and make any sort of sense, she simply reached out and rested her fingers on the girl's forearm. The girl allowed the sketch book to slip from her grip and she looked at Bella with a tentative gaze. "It's not what you're looking for, is it?"

Bella drew a sharp breath. She had thought that she might let out a kind of giggle, or a nervous chuckle at the very least, but she was left only with having given the impression of a sudden shock. She managed to find her voice. "This is *absolutely* what I'm looking for."

The girl stared at her for a few seconds, and then blinked, as if to break the spell. "Oh," she replied. "That's . . . good."

Finally, Bella managed to get a grip on herself. "No, it's *more* than good." She glanced down at the sketch books, almost unable to restrain herself from flipping through the second one, to see what sort of wonders featured there . . . whether she might take in yet more overlaps from the world of her dreams and the real world which the girl — *Cassandra* — had committed to the page. "They're wonderful."

The girl smiled more widely and then — as if she felt she was overstepping the mark — she looked about the kitchen nervously, as if in hope of encountering something to distract her from the uncomfortable moment. "Are you just moving in here?"

Still focused on the sketch books lying before her, Bella nearly missed the question. She looked at the girl again. "How'd you guess?"

"Well, you know, there's . . . nothing here."

Bella grinned. "I know — a disaster, isn't it?"

The girl continued to look about her. Then she said, "I don't know, it seems like paradise to me. I'm sharing a three-bedroom house with eight other people."

"Where're you working?"

"In a pub."

Bella nodded to herself. "I was always a waitress myself — cafes and restaurants; they were my domain."

The two of them giggled nervously at Bella's half-joke.

"What would you think of coming to stay here?" Bella asked, and then, realising just how forward this might sound — just how *quickly* things might be moving — she drew herself back. "I mean, I think it would be best . . . at least to start out . . . so that we can work together."

But the girl seemed to have slipped away. Her attention was off in some other direction, staring out towards the back garden.

Bella followed her gaze, expecting to see Florianette's ghost gradually picking its way up the garden path. What Bella *did* see was no less frightening. A stranger. Walking towards the back door. They had let themselves in through the garden gate.

Bella's senses returned to her. Her first reaction was to turn to Cassandra, with some sort of a maternal instinct. "Wait here."

Bella strode through the gloomy kitchen and out to the garden. She realised she was only wearing a pair of slippers when she trod on the damp grass and felt an unpleasant wetness through the soles of her feet. Finally, she realised who it was.

Robert.

Florianette's *son*.

It was no wonder Bella had been taken by surprise — that she had been brought into mind of phantoms. Robert's whole face was gaunt; his cheeks dug out and his eyes set back so far in their sockets that they seemed almost as if they were retreating down a pair of bottomless pits. He wore a crumpled suit and had a week's worth of stubble.

He took another few steps towards Bella, his eyes meeting hers. It was then that she realised he had sapphire-blue eyes. He stopped a couple of steps away from her. And then spoke her name. "Bella."

The two of them stared at one another for the longest time. And then — it happened so quickly . . . just like a dream. He closed the gap between them, planting his lips up against hers. His lips were gentle and his beard stubble was wiry but soft. They stood like that for what felt like over a minute. Bella felt sparks shoot through her stomach and down her legs. When Robert withdrew, he appeared to have remembered himself. He was looking over Bella's shoulder to where Cassandra stood at the back door. When he looked at Bella, his eyes widened — a silent apology perhaps? — and then he retreated, heading out of the garden, and to the back alley which ran alongside the house.

Only when the garden gate rattled shut was the spell broken.

FLEDGLING STEPS

*I*t took Bella the best part of a week to get over just what had happened between herself and Robert. For one thing, she had had no idea that he would ever return to Normonswold. With his mother gone, why would he? Had it simply been a case of Robert wishing to see her home one final time? Had he heard the rumours of Bella buying the house and turning it to her own uses? And if that was the case, then was he angry about it — did he *disapprove* of what she was doing? The only interpretation Bella could gather from what had happened between them in the back garden was that he didn't mind *all* that much . . . or maybe he had just entered a kind of shock. She certainly knew she had.

Following their first meeting, Cassandra had got on the train, gone to fetch her things from the bedroom she shared in London, and come right back to live with Bella in one of the spare bedrooms of Molinaar's Cottage.

As the two of them set about unpacking a delivery of flat-pack kitchen furniture — the long-promised chairs and table — Cassandra proved herself a lot more conversational than when they had first met. Although it seemed strange, in the days that had gone by so far, there had hardly been a chance for them to learn about one another. Any conversation they did have was really just a superficial entry point into speaking about the work which awaited them. Bella wasn't sure whether this might've been her fault above all else. She only knew that she couldn't *help* speaking with Cassandra about Humble Greetings whenever she got the sniff of an opportunity. As they unpacked the furniture, however, it appeared that Cassandra was tiring of the Humble conversations and was determined to unpack other topics.

Cassandra went about fitting a slender wooden leg to the base panel of one of the chairs. She closed one eye and poked her tongue out as she did so, giving her a much younger look than her true age. When she had successfully made the connection between chair leg and base panel, she glanced up at Bella. "How long have you lived in Normonswold?"

"I grew up here."

"When did you move to London?"

"Oh" — Bella remained standing pensively, as she had done for the past ten minutes, over the table lying flat on the kitchen floor, unable quite to suck up the courage to start on putting the legs into the anointed slots — "I was about your age."

Cassandra nodded to herself, clearly finding this logical. "And why did you come back?"

There was the question which Bella had dreaded, and yet she found it an easy one to answer, at least speaking to Cassandra. "I wanted to start my own company — Humble."

Again, Cassandra nodded.

Who would've thought that speaking aloud the truth would make so much sense to someone else?

"And this house?" Cassandra went on, and then paused, as if she was about to tread on insensitive territory.

"Go on," Bella prompted.

"Did you buy this house after you sold your place in London?"

Bella grinned widely. Then she shook her head. "I'm sorry, but even a *successful* copy-writer, as I liked to think of myself, doesn't earn the sort of money which permits them to *buy* somewhere of their own in London. Not without a hefty mortgage, anyway. Living there doesn't allow for any sort of savings, either, really."

"So," Cassandra continued, "how did you . . ."

"Find the funds for this place?"

Cassandra pressed her lips together, squeezing all the blood out of them. But then she nodded.

Bella met her eye. "I came to an agreement with my mother — a *payment* plan, you might call it."

"Does your mother approve of it — of what you're trying to do?"

" 'Approve' is a strong word . . . I would say that she's seen what I've been doing to myself — and my *career* — for the past ten years, and she wanted to step in . . . pull me out of the fiery wreckage, perhaps. Give me a chance to douse myself with water." From Cassandra's expression, Bella could see she was losing her — it was an expression Bella had seen so often while pitching in meetings . . . one which told her right away and unequivocally that she had lost the sale.

"Still," Cassandra said, with a shrug, "I wish my parents would do something like that for me. I mean" — she met Bella's eye — "I don't expect them to understand that I just want to . . . just want to *draw* . . . or, well, I suppose that I *do* expect them to understand that's what I want to do and that I'll most likely be unable to support myself doing it. But, to get started, to make a success of it, I just . . . just . . ."

"Need a little push?"

Cassandra nodded then smiled. "Yeah, that's right." She glanced about the house and then grinned wider still. "This is quite a *big* push."

Cassandra and Bella selected a room facing out into the back garden to be their study. They worked together to unpack the various drawing supplies, and the pair of computers, and they set about assembling a *pair* of desks. One thing was for certain, and it was that Cassandra was a much defter hand at slotting together flat-pack furniture than Bella was. Perhaps for this ability alone, Bella had made a good decision in bringing her on board.

By evening, when Bella had lit a few candles and set them in the night-time garden, the house looked far homier than it had done at any point previously. And it felt — if Bella hadn't already convinced herself it was so — that Humble Greetings was on the right track. Bella had just got to thinking about what she and Cassandra were going to eat that evening when she heard the — now-all-too-familiar — *thump-thump-thump* at the front door.

As Bella went to answer, she supposed that it would most likely be her mother, or perhaps even Dorothy/Kieran who had popped by for a chat and a cup of tea . . . even Adiema had stopped by a few times to run her eye over just what Bella was doing to Molinaar's Cottage. However, when Bella answered the door, it wasn't her mother, or Dorothy/Kieran or even Adiema who was standing there.

It was Harriet.

Harriet Tumblebeach.

"Can we talk, Bella?"

Bella found herself dumbstruck, so she simply stepped back from the door and allowed Harriet to walk in through the gap. As Bella took in Harriet, she saw that she was wearing an elegant, long silver-grey coat with an icy-blue scarf tucked in about the upturned collar. She had on a pair of knee-high boots. Something about her appearance — her *presence* — put Bella in mind of royalty. Ever since they had been school girls, she had always believed that Harriet was the *pretty* one . . .

Although it took almost everything in Bella not to blurt out, *What do you want?* Bella managed it. She supposed that despite all her time spent in London with some of the Rudest People in the World, she still maintained her Small Town Manners.

Harriet stepped into the kitchen, and Bella felt somewhat glad that Cassandra had decided to go upstairs to organise her bedroom. It would've been . . . *tricky* to explain exactly what her relationship with Harriet really was . . . an added complication which Harriet really didn't need right now.

Harriet hovered for several seconds, as if deciding whether or not she had done the right thing in coming here — although Bella still had no idea just *why* she had come — before settling on one of the chairs at the head of the kitchen table. Now sat down, she hesitated another moment before shrugging off her coat and hanging it on the back of her chair. She glanced up at Bella, meeting her eye, her gaze containing something sharp — something *fierce*.

"Cup of tea?" Bella asked, still insufferably polite.

"Yes, please."

Bella was glad to have something to busy her hands as she went about putting the kettle onto boil. The silence was positively frozen as they sat listening to the bubbling water. When Bella had poured out the cups and taken Bella's over to where she sat at the kitchen table, she realised there would be no further dawdling allowed. This was the moment she had feared . . . well, ever since the Incident.

Harriet nodded to the cup as Bella placed it before her, as if the tea had materialised all by itself, and she was thanking it duly. Harriet peered into the tea for several seconds before glancing up. "Your mum knows."

Bella said nothing in reply. She waited for Harriet to go on.

"She has been very supportive of me . . ."

Bella supposed this was some sort of a guarded allusion to the fact that Harriet had attended that little 'gathering' of her mother's — just what was supportive about getting drunk in the afternoon with a trio of fifty-somethings, she had no idea. But, then again, Bella could never say she had been in the same situation as Harriet.

"You have to understand how damaging what happened was for me. And the way that you were able to — you know — just sort of . . . *walk away* . . . I won't lie, I did hate you for a long time. Whenever you would come home for Christmas, for the holidays, whatever else, I would hear the stories about how successful you were being in the city — about your job, your *boyfriends* — and I wouldn't know what to do with the information . . . it produced a tiny ball of hate in my stomach."

Bella held Harriet's stare, unsure where she was going with this, and yet knowing exactly where this would end up. Where this *had* to end up.

"I felt like a victim for such a long time, as if I was someone who just had stuff *happen* to me. That was why I could never move away from Normonswold . . . that was why I never had the courage to do what you did . . . to *escape*."

Bella felt a skitter run up her spine.

Harriet bowed her head and a single tear ran down her cheek. After a few seconds, she reached up and wiped it away, irritated. Then she looked at Bella with a newfound ferocity. "When I saw you that night. On the doorstep. With my *dad* . . . I thought . . . well, there was nothing else for me to think. That was the end. The end for me. And . . . I . . . thought it was just your idea of *fun* . . . just your idea . . . your idea . . ."

At this point Harriet broke down completely. She simply couldn't hold her raw emotions back any longer. She propped her elbows on the kitchen table and sobbed into her palms. To begin with, Bella was at a loss about what precisely she should do. And then her Girl Sense steered her in the right direction — as it so often did.

She rounded the table, coming up behind Harriet. Although it felt like a danger comparable with setting bare feet on hot coals, she wrapped her arms about her and squeezed her to her chest.

To begin with, Harriet resisted.

In the end, though, she relented.

And she allowed Bella to squeeze hold of her tightly.

After a long while had passed — ten, fifteen minutes of silence? — Bella heard footsteps on the stairs. When she glanced up, she saw Cassandra standing in the kitchen doorway, looking thoroughly confused. Catching Bella's eye, she said, "Oh, I'm sorry — I thought you were alone . . . I mean, I thought your visitor had . . . had *gone*." And, as if the act of correcting this social faux pas was now complete, Cassandra turned on her heel and disappeared back up the stairs to her bedroom.

Bella gave Harriet a little respite from her vice-like grip. Then she stood back from her. She knew it wasn't her time to speak, that this was Harriet's moment, that she had waited *so* long to have this opportunity. To set things right between the two of them.

And it was Bella's time to listen.

Not to run away.

"It was such a special night, wasn't it?" Harriet said, her eyes on Bella, the question directed at herself more than anyone. "And it was just how I had hoped it would go — that after the school leavers' dance, we ditched our dates and set off together. Just the two of us. I remember how we slipped off our heels and went down to the creek. That we dipped our toes in the freezing-cold water. It was so refreshing. It'd been so stuffy all day. I remember how we were talking nonstop about our plans to go to the city. How we were going to live together, and help support one another. In sickness and in health, that sort of a deal."

Harriet blew out her cheeks, releasing a large quantity of hot air.

As if she was physically expelling bad memories.

Literally *clearing the air* between the two of them.

"I was just so happy — you can't imagine — when the two of us returned to my house, when you were seeing me off at the door. And then . . . and then . . . well, I thought it was only normal — just a matter of *concern* . . . but . . ."

Harriet squeezed her eyes together all the tighter.

Bella willed her on silently.

She couldn't stop now.

She had to *keep going.*

This would be difficult, but revisiting precisely what had happened was the only way of truly holding the actions up to the light. The only right way to *deal* with them. And Harriet was so close now. Just a little way further to go . . . and then the two of them would be free.

"When my dad decided to walk you home, I don't know what I was thinking in following you. I suppose that it was a pang of jealousy, even then, even though I couldn't possibly have *known* what was going . . . what was going to happen." Harriet shook her head. There were no tears now. She seemed to be seeing things more clearly — more matter-of-factly. "I was bare-foot . . . I remember that . . . and there was the vague thought that my dad should've, well, you know, taken you by car. The walk's not long — what, ten minutes? — but I thought he could've at the very least driven you . . . even though the night wasn't particularly cold . . . I suppose it was just a nice night for walking . . ."

Harriet looked away, staring into the empty air again, her chin pressed into her palm. She breathed in deeply again, apparently preparing herself for the final assault on her memories. "When you got to the driveway, I was certain that the two of you had heard me, that you *knew* I was following on your heels. I thought that you might turn around and surprise me at any second. And then, when you reached the doorstep of your house — of your *mother's* house — and my dad . . . when he . . . leaned in . . . I thought that it was all part of the joke. I expected the two of you to turn to me, scream out in laughter, or whatever. But, in the end, I was the one who screamed."

Of that much, Bella was sure. She could still hear the scream which'd rattled about her skull as she had finally summoned up the strength to force Harriet's father away. To begin with she had convinced herself that it was some kind of a phantom which dwelled in the trees surrounding the driveway. But then she had caught sight of Harriet retreating — the soles of her bare feet throwing up dirt and gravel as she disappeared around the bend.

As she disappeared from Bella's life.

They had been so close.

They had wasted so many years.

And all because of a man . . . it didn't matter that the man had been Harriet's father, or that Bella had never had *any* sort of feelings towards him, the Incident had sliced through the fibres of their relationship like a razorblade.

And now it was Bella's turn to cry.

THE RISING STORM

*R*obert looked across the unmarked terrain. It was boggy, and there were few trees. Robert was no landscaper, let alone an architect, but one thing was for certain, his client, Lord Charles Knightly, had his work cut out if he truly wished to transform this area into an all-inclusive golf resort.

As a bitterly cold north wind blew across the moors, Robert popped the collar of his jacket, and tightened the scarf about his neck. He could feel Woss pressing in against his calf, shuddering from the cold. It had to take a special kind of cold for Woss to be hinting for them to get back in the car. Deciding that getting in the car was the most sensible course of action right now — dogs were man's best friend, after all — Robert meandered his way back across the soggy fields and through the several gates to where he had parked.

Like always, Woss rode up front, leaping onto the passenger seat so that he could see exactly what was going on. Robert held the car steady as they made progress along the winding lanes, away from the fields.

As his mind drifted with the grisly grey skies overhead, and the feeling of damp coldness which seemed even to seep into his car, he couldn't help but think back to the rashness of what he had done just over a week ago . . . how he had effectively *broken into* his mother's house — into what had *been* his mother's back garden — and he had found Bella Miles there. The whole act had been pure improvisation. He recalled how he had just parked up his car by the side of the road, and how he had got out, his mind drawing a blank. Before he'd known it, he was pushing his way through the back garden gate, and then treading across the grass, seeing Bella there . . . the most divine sight he had ever seen . . . something — well, there was no other way of putting it — *dreamlike*.

Robert eased the car over a series of ruts, returning to the road which led back to the village of Normonswold. He stopped at the intersection and stared out ahead for the longest time. It was almost as if he could see the nightmare which'd haunted him for so long. When he had parked up the car and gone in through the back garden gate, he had seen that darkened corridor from his dreams. And there had been no option but to keep going.

Bella had been at the end of the corridor.

What did it mean?

Robert turned to look at Woss, sat upright on the passenger seat. He was staring longingly at him, waiting to see what their next move would be, trusting Robert without question — trusting Robert *implicitly*.

Right as Robert's thoughts swam deeper and deeper, his mobile began to buzz. He gave himself until it rang a third time and then answered — ready to lose himself in his work once again.

Lord Charles Knightly wasn't the calibre of man accustomed to taking public transport — Robert had been able to intuit that much in their first meeting. And so, as Robert stood on the station platform waiting for Lord Charles, he knew that Lord Charles was likely to be in a foul mood before they even began. Just how Lord Charles had contrived to end up taking a train — rather than having someone drive him — Robert had no idea. As the train carriage slid into view at Unthorpe Station, Robert had already pictured Lord Charles emerging red-faced and furious, looking for someone onto whom he could let out his anger.

It was nothing but a profound surprise, then, when Lord Charles positively *bounded* down from the train. His fresh-faced, thirty-something assistant bobbed on his heels, clutching the suitcases.

As Lord Charles came closer, Robert saw that he was grinning from ear to ear, and that while there was no doubt he was red of complexion, it had nothing to do with fury, but . . . pure *joy*.

Robert was so taken aback, so surprised to see this version of Lord Charles, as compared to the one he had become acquainted to in the city, that he was of half a mind to get in touch with the police to report an imposter.

Soon, however, as Lord Charles set about pumping Robert's hand while imploring, "Robert! *Robert* m'boy!" he realised that there was no explanation to be had, other than that which was most obvious. This *was* Lord Charles.

Robert had to peel his fingers free from Lord Charles's grip — before they got themselves broken, more than anything. As he led Lord Charles and his assistant to where he had parked up, Robert was still struggling to get his head around how his expectations had been completely turned on their head. Robert was hardly thinking straight when he opened up the driver's side of the car only to have Woss leap out from within.

Woss jumped up at Lord Charles, pressing his muddy paws against the man's spotless suit trousers. If Lord Charles found Woss at all objectionable, then he made a very good job of hiding the fact. Lord Charles embraced Woss.

When Lord Charles finally straightened up, Robert was convinced that there was a tear or two in the man's eye. "Robert! You didn't *tell* me you had a *dog!*"

Robert thought back to their dour first meeting in some anonymous, slick bar in a city skyscraper and how Lord Charles had been serious, removed, *businesslike* in procuring Robert's services. There hadn't been a lot — *any* — scope for chat of a personal kind.

"This is Woss," Robert said, although the introduction seemed somewhat moot at this stage. Woss and Lord Charles were already getting on famously.

Robert couldn't help but notice how the assistant was somewhat more reluctant about diving in to greet Woss, that he preferred to hang back, still clutching the suitcases.

Once they had packed the suitcases into the car boot, George — as Lord Charles's assistant turned out to be called — took up his place in the back seat, alongside Woss, while Lord Charles sat up front with Robert. Although George and Lord Charles still wore their overcoats, Robert was pleased to see that he had not overdressed in deciding to wear a suit that day. Even despite the raucous meeting, Lord Charles and George were both dressed for business. As this thought crossed Robert's mind again, he couldn't help but sneak another sidelong glance at Lord Charles, just to check that the man was *really* smiling. When their gaze met, Lord Charles seemed unable to help himself, he burst out in yet another bristling grin and slapped Robert on the thigh. Robert was so surprised, he almost drove the car into the grassy bank at the side of the road.

"So, so *wonderful* to get out into the countryside, isn't it?"

Robert smiled back politely and squeezed the steering wheel, turning his focus to the road ahead, and any rabbits which might potentially think it a good idea to dash out in front of his car tyres. "I . . . uh, my mother certainly loved it here." Even as the words made their way past Robert's lips, he couldn't stop himself from wincing. He blamed the situation — how Lord Charles's mood had thoroughly thrown him off balance . . . it was and had always been his policy to never, ever, under any circumstance, mix business with personal affairs.

This statement seemed to give Lord Charles pause for thought. "Your mother?" he said, as if he was surprised Robert had a mother at all. Then Lord Charles blinked and his smile scaled back to a mere shadow of what it had been a few seconds before. "I am sorry, Robert, I had no idea. Did she . . . pass away recently?"

"Sir?" Lord Charles's assistant put in from the back seat, from where he was being wilily surveyed by Woss.

Lord Charles leaned back to take in his assistant.

"Mr Rutherford's mother was Florianette Rutherford, of Nightwalker."

Even despite the situation, Robert had the rush of feeling to correct Lord Charles's assistant, to tell him that she had also run Modern Styles in the village of Normonswold, and this was truly where her heart lay — but he managed to keep himself from saying anything further.

"I am sorry," Lord Charles said, meeting Robert's eye and looking sincere. "I really had no idea." A slight smile lifted the corners of his mouth. "You know, it never occurred for me to think . . . well, *fashion designer* . . . *accountant* . . . the idea just never occurred."

And although Robert felt himself breaking up on the inside, he managed to squeeze the shadow of a smile out of his lips — a smile of the bereaved — and drove the car onward, headed without pause for Normonswold village.

13

TIME AND PEACE

*B*ella had to admit that she was nothing short of *thrilled* at how the first Humble Greetings designs were shaping up. It was better than anything she ever could've imagined.

Cassandra was better than she ever could have imagined.

In the end, they had settled on producing an initial run of five greetings cards. This was where Bella would pin down the Humble ideology — what it was that consumers could expect from the brand. Whenever Bella caught herself thinking in this way about her heart project, she had to ward away concerns afresh each time that she had simply swapped one joyless job for another. Whereas Humble was about freedom and creativity, the Old World — to Bella's mind at least — represented restriction and paint-by-numbers. She had to take measures to ensure these divisions remained. Many times, as she and Cassandra worked side by side, attempting to produce some design or other — to capture the essence of whatever idea it was Bella happened to have floating about inside her brain — Bella had to scold herself for pushing them too hard . . . for trying to *force* something to take shape, as she had so often done back in the city.

And it hardly helped that the whole village was abuzz with Lord Charles Knightly's arrival. It had been impossible for Bella to avoid the news — *gossip?* — that he was currently residing at the Thicket Arms Inn just down the road. A couple of times, Bella had seen Lord Charles, and his ever-present assistant, strolling through the village, taking in the sights.

In actual fact, like everything else which came to Normonswold from London, Lord Charles was an unpleasant reminder of the world which she had left behind. Although she had never met Lord Charles himself, she had worked on a marketing campaign for one of his many companies.

That had been an *especially* joyless experience.

Throughout her time working on the campaign, she recalled how the person she was responsible to — some snooty, Oxbridge-educated snob — had constantly revised whatever she would put forward as copy for the ads they were designing. Whenever Bella had attempted to step in and professionally defend whatever liberty she had taken with the English language to get her message across, said snob would justify his corrections by claiming that they came directly from Lord Charles . . . and despite the ridiculousness of such claims, Bella couldn't help but feel a tiny itch of frustration each and every time she saw Lord Charles and his assistant 'out and about' in Normonswold. Perhaps the true test of the success of Humble would be whether or not these things about her old life continued to bother her after she had made a success of her new one.

She *would* make a success of her new life . . . anything else was unthinkable.

Where Lord Charles was concerned, the village was swept up with his plans to construct an all-inclusive golf resort on the swampy land surrounding. People's reactions ranged from disbelief to outright *anger* that Lord Charles had the nerve to do something so base as *buy up* property and do what he wanted with it. And it was only made worse by Lord Charles's outward manner — that he was just so *damn* affable.

Bella, though, did her best to put Village Concerns out of her mind. She and Cassandra would pull the blinds on what had once been the Modern Styles shop floor — and which had now been converted into their studio. In the future, Bella planned to throw open the blinds, to reveal their studio to the world. And she was of course keen to take advantage of the spring and summer sun in the next year.

As Christmas closed in, Lord Charles's constant presence in and around the village soon became an outdated topic of conversation. People turned their minds to the far more important matter of the Christmas decorations, and especially the Christmas lights. Bella had always made a conscious effort to keep herself at an arm's length from all things connected to local politics — and that definitely included village events. She knew only too well how fights could start over something so simple as the choice of white light bulbs over yellow. And Bella had enough choices to be getting on with, what with all the creative work she was putting into Humble. All the same, it was difficult for Bella to keep on working when Christmas Eve rolled around.

With Cassandra having gone home for Christmas, Bella remained in the Humble studio, scribbling away at some phrases to fit Cassandra's drawings, drafting and redrafting — just trying to find the *right* word — when she heard the giveaway sing-song of carollers.

Back in the city, there was a sure-fire method of dealing with *carollers*.

Ignoring them.

It was safe to say that this was the most reliable method of dealing with just about any given issue in the city.

As Bella continued to work, pressing her fingers into her temple and staring at the words she had scribbled to fit the current drawing, she traced the carollers' progress, making their way from the front door of Molinaar's Cottage to being right outside the storefront of what had been Modern Styles . . . pretty soon, the carollers were bellowing away in their best approximation of a melody right against the glass.

Unable to continue with her work any longer, Bella laid her pencil down and took a few steps. That was when she realised that the carollers' voices were not getting any quieter. In short, that they were continuing to sing right outside the window. As if they were directing their songs right at her.

As if . . .

Bella whipped through the undecorated cottage. There simply hadn't been time to go through the whole rigmarole of buying baubles, tinsel and lights. She had consciously decided to give Christmas a miss this year. What with her planning on running a greetings card business Bella had decided that she would get enough of Christmas for a lifetime.

When she opened the door, she was taken aback by the icy chill which rushed in.

In the darkness, she realised that a faint layer of snow had settled across the landscape. It must've happened that afternoon. Bella hadn't opened the curtains since that morning. Her attention focused on the foreground. On the carollers. One by one, they ceased their singing.

"Well, about time!" Bella's mother said, stepping forward from where she stood between Harriet, Adiema and Dorothy/Kieran — who was definitely in his Dorothy guise today wearing a quite fetching Mrs Claus outfit, complete with sparkly silver earrings, a pair of ruby-red, knee-high boots, and with a sleek, leather handbag dangling from the crook of his elbow.

As her mother threw her arms about her, Bella saw that the three other carollers were just as red in the face. Despite all of them being well wrapped up — with earmuffs, or beanie hats squeezed over the tops of their heads — they were shifting from one foot to the other in order to get warm.

"Uh," Bella said, still caught off guard by the sight of other people here when she had been so diligently off in her own little world, "would you like to come in?"

Her mother allowed Bella just enough free rein so that she could get a glance over her shoulder, into the cottage. And, with a sigh, her mother said, "I don't *think* so, dear. Not very Christmassy in there, is it?"

And Bella felt her mother tugging at her, ever so gently encouraging her out through the doorway, and into the frozen night.

"Mum!" Bella said. "I've nothing on my feet!"

It was then that her mother deigned to glance down, to see that — *indeed* — Bella was only in socks. She cocked her head to one side. "Two minutes," she said. "We're going to the pub. Lord Charles is throwing a big party. Free drink, Bella!"

From the looks of their faces, and the hip flask she had seen Adiema subtly passing to Dorothy, Bella wondered if 'free drink' was really what they all most needed at this particular moment in time. Bella flirted with the idea of closing the front door behind them — *locking it* — and then going off to hide in an upstairs room. In the end, though, she decided that would be too cruel an act to play on a group of people whose only crime was in wanting to bring a little warmth and happiness into her life.

Bella rushed upstairs, foraged about for her winter coat — which she hadn't put to much use — before bounding back down, headed for the front hall. It was just as she was about to turn the corner, to go out into the night, that something tickled her . . . there was no other way to describe the sensation. It was as if someone had jiggled a feather in her gut.

She made a swift diversion, headed back into her studio — what had been the Modern Styles shop floor.

Her focus fell onto the card which Cassandra had drawn about a month ago and which Bella had left blank inside. It sat on a shelf, holding court over the whole studio.

The design was simple, and it really had nothing at all to do with Humble — the style just didn't fit the aesthetic Bella was going for. And then there was the subject matter. Cassandra had drawn a picture-perfect rendering of Molinaar's Cottage, all covered in snow. Bella had flirted with the idea of getting a batch printed and sending them out to people as Christmas cards, but, in the end, she had decided against it.

There just wasn't enough time.

And just who would she actually send them out to?

After all, she was doing her best to keep her current business venture a secret from all those she had known in her past life in the city.

She snatched up a pen, flattened the card, scribbled a greeting inside, and slipped it into her coat pocket.

14

CHRISTMAS EVE

*T*he warmth within the Thicket Arms Inn was most welcoming. Tinsel and glittering silver and gold lights hung from the support beams of the pub ceiling. People thronged about the bar. With the Christmas shopping all done and — Bella supposed — the food all waiting to be put in the oven early the next morning, the residents of Normonswold were taking a well-earned rest before Festive Mayhem overtook everything tomorrow.

The smell of wood smoke and ale overwhelmed everything. There was a certain sharp odour of whisky which kept wafting up Bella's nostrils. Her investigation was soon brought to an abrupt conclusion when she felt a nudge on the arm and a grinning Dorothy was offering her the hipflask they had been passing around surreptitiously on the doorstep an hour or so earlier. Although Bella wasn't usually a whisky girl, she decided to make an exception this particular evening, knocking back the hipflask and taking down a healthy measure.

"Good girl!" Dorothy said, clapping her on the back.

When Bella passed the flask onto Harriet, the whole world seemed to be grinning at her. She slumped back into the overly soft cushions and allowed her eyes to slip out of focus. All the Christmas colours blurred together, the lights all becoming warped, crazy stars, bursting apart. She felt strange at that particular moment. Warm on the inside. And then she realised what it was . . . for the first time in a very long time she was actually . . . *happy*.

As Bella absorbed all that was happening around her, she lost herself in not really thinking about anything at all. It was such a long time since she had just stopped and allowed her mind to relax. Every single morning for the past few months, she had woken up with a firm idea of what needed to be achieved that particular day.

Now, though, she realised she had been pushing herself too hard.

She had been *forcing* things.

As she sat there, she wondered about Cassandra. Had she realised Bella was getting carried away? Would she even come back to Normonswold after Christmas?

Bella dismissed this concern from her mind.

It was stupid to think about it now.

She was most likely making mountains out of molehills.

"Now, I can't say I've seen you out and about during my perambulations."

Bella returned to reality with a *thump*. She glanced up. Saw that it was Lord Charles Knightly himself. She watched on as his assistant helped Lord Charles from his jacket, unpeeling the scarf about his neck too. Lord Charles apparently saw Bella's lack of reply as an invitation for him to sit with them — no matter how much Bella would've liked him to go just about any place else. He shifted uncomfortably close to her, and it felt as if there was nothing Bella could do to subtly extricate herself from him. When she looked up at her mother, to Dorothy, Adiema, and Harriet, they had all consciously shifted away — each of them in turn shooting her a 'subtle' glance, keeping a good eye on what was going on with the local celebrity and Bella.

"George here" — he jerked his thumb back to indicate his assistant — "tells me that you've got a little venture going in the village."

Bella felt her whole body lock up at the idea. She drew in a sharp breath, feeling that Lord Charles was cramping her into the corner of the pub. As if there was no escape. It was then that she felt his hand on her thigh. Lord Charles leaned into her, his breath impossibly hot, and rancid-smelling.

"Greetings cards, is that right?"

Bella felt him squeeze her thigh tighter.

"Well," he continued, in a husky voice, "those would look just wonderful in a gift shop, shouldn't you think? When I finally get my own venture off the ground, I would certainly welcome the opportunity of doing business with you . . ."

It was only after a second or so that Bella interpreted the lingering silence as Lord Charles's signal for her to give him her name.

"Bella Miles."

"*Miss* Miles. Ah!"

It was then that Bella allowed herself to look up — when she allowed herself the risk of taking her eye off Lord Charles for a second.

Her heart skipped a beat as he walked through the door.

Robert.

There was a terrifying moment when he looked about the whole of the pub, and Bella conjured the childish nightmare scenario that he would never even see that she was there at all — that he wouldn't be able to *save* her.

But then — as if she had called out to him in a sharp voice — Robert's eyes snapped onto her. They were so serious for a second, and she did wonder if he had worked out what was going on. Realised exactly where Lord Charles's wandering hand was . . . And then Robert gave a warm smile and began to make his way over. She saw that tonight he had tied his shoulder-length hair back into a businesslike ponytail.

Lord Charles shifted in his seat and Bella took the opportunity to release her thigh from his grasp, standing and then taking up a place in a chair across from him. She made a conscious effort not to look at Lord Charles, although, with Robert — and, she saw, Woss — here now, she realised that wasn't going to be as difficult a prospect as it seemed.

"Merry Christmas," Robert said, smiling at them all, and then — her heart aflutter — settling on Bella.

Heat rose in Bella's cheeks and she couldn't help noticing that her mother, Adiema, Harriet and Dorothy were all looking at her with wide grins. Although Bella had told precisely no one about what had gone on with Robert, she couldn't help but wonder if Cassandra might've perhaps leaked something about what'd gone on between them that night . . . when Robert had come in through the back garden and kissed her.

On instinct, Bella looked to Robert, maybe expecting him to be swooping in for another kiss right there and then. But he remained focused on Lord Charles, across the table, who — Bella couldn't help but notice — had just received a pint of ale.

Lord Charles grinned with delight at the liquid within the

glass, turned gold by the lights inside the pub, and then, with a slight stumble — kept from becoming any worse by his assistant — he got to his feet.

Lord Charles's presence was such that he hardly needed to do much more than clear his throat in order to bring the whole of the Thicket Arms to silence. Or maybe it was just a polite reverence brought on by simple respect for the person who was funding this evening of free-flowing drink and festive cheer. As Lord Charles spoke, Bella couldn't help but marvel at how calm and in control his voice was despite his tipsiness.

"It was with great pleasure that I stumbled across Normonswold, in the search for somewhere to lay my legacy, and it delights me to think how kindly the people here have taken to me. It's not often in small towns that residents have a positive attitude to change — they want everything to stay the same — but I can't help thinking that this particular place" — and here, with an electrifying spark in her gut, he looked directly at Bella — "things are very different indeed."

Bella forced herself to meet Lord Charles's stare. She had never backed down from a fight in her life, and she wasn't going to do so now . . . whether or not Lord Charles bought drinks for the entire country on Christmas Eve.

Lord Charles broke off the stare and his familiar, bumbling, bright smile returned as he continued to address the pub. "I have to admit that I feel nothing less than a fellow Normonswoldian this evening and I can only thank you — on the most joyful of all nights — for having taken me so kindly to your hearts." He raised his glass. "Cheers!"

A chorus of *Cheers!* greeted Lord Charles's own declaration.

Lord Charles continued to hold court late into Christmas Eve. Bella took her chance to skulk away and join her mother, Adiema, Harriet and Dorothy while Lord Charles's attention was diverted by the village people, asking after plans for his golf resort.

Bella took no little pleasure in observing how the villagers' questions gradually — one after the next — turned Lord Charles's previously beaming grin into a slight frown. She supposed that Lord Charles might have been a little premature in proclaiming himself a 'Normonswoldian' . . . especially when those in this area referred to themselves as 'Normonslanders'.

Although on the surface it should've been something that really didn't matter at all, Bella couldn't help but think that Lord Charles had only succeeded in driving a stake in the ground, declaring more clearly than he ever could have done, that he was an outsider . . . and what was more, someone who couldn't care *less* for the village and its residents.

Indeed, along with Lord Charles's disappearing smile, the whole atmosphere of the pub seemed to have become dampened somewhat. As people dribbled out one by one, it was only with a sense of duty and politeness that they shook Lord Charles by the hand and thanked him for the drinks. She supposed that Lord Charles was learning that the village wouldn't be so easily bought, after all.

About half an hour before closing time, Lord Charles looked to his assistant, and — without a word ever needing to be passed between the two of them — the assistant went off to fetch Lord Charles's coat. This was the moment Bella had been dreading. She had impressed in her imagination the idea that Lord Charles would take the farewell as another golden groping opportunity. So she snuck off to the toilets.

When she returned to the pub, she was glad to see that Lord

Charles was gone — his assistant too — but she felt an icy pang in her heart to notice that Robert was nowhere to be seen. It was then that she recalled the card she had slipped into her coat pocket. Her heart racing, she lay the card down on the table where Lord Charles had been sitting. She padded her coat and located the pen she always kept in the inside pocket. She stared at the card another moment, and then — inspiration striking her — she opened it up and scribbled her message within. That done, she hustled out of the pub, not so much as glancing over at her mother and the others for fear that they would call her back and she would lose this moment. There was no time to waste.

Outside, it was snowing heavily now. It settled in layers. The wind was still and the night was crisp. Her breath billowed in clouds from her nostrils and mouth. She located Robert almost instantly. It wasn't as she'd feared.

He was alone.

Lord Charles had gone *elsewhere*.

Her heart pulsing in her eardrums, she jogged after him, seeing how Woss — plodding along faithfully at his master's heel — glanced back over his shoulder, and, seeing her there, began to wag his tail and stare at her with wide eyes. This caught Robert's attention. First he looked to Woss, and then he glanced back to Bella.

She stopped her approach.

For the longest moment, Bella convinced herself that Robert wouldn't say anything to her. That he would just turn around and keep on going . . . well, to wherever it was that he was bedding down for that particular evening.

Unwilling to allow Robert even the smallest of chances of escaping her clutches, she held up the card she had brought with her. She held it out to him but he didn't see it right away — his eyes remaining focused on her. Finally, he looked down.

The only light on the lane was from the golden lamps which illuminated the pub sign. But it was enough for Robert to get the general idea. He reached out for the card. "For me?"

"Uh-huh."

He pouted slightly as he took it from her, holding up the picture and examining it in the gloom. When he recognised what the image represented, he smiled lightly. And Bella was certain that she saw the vaguest glean of tears shining off his eyes. In a moment, however, the tears — if they had even been there at all — were gone.

"Very kind of you," he replied.

"Open it."

Robert continued to hold the card away from him, as if he was planning on returning it to Bella, as if it *belonged* to her . . . but he did as she said, peeling back the front cover. He stared for a long time at what Bella had hastily written inside.

"To remember," he said, his voice a husky whisper.

Bella drew in a breath, right down to the bottoms of her lungs. Although the snow was falling harder than ever, she felt nothing but warmth within her chest. Her cheeks were glowing, but not with the cold . . . no, they were *glowing* with happiness.

Robert turned the card over in his hands another time. "I . . . don't know . . ."

But Bella decided she had heard enough and she lurched forward, pressing her lips up against his. There was very little that Robert could do except for allow her to overwhelm him. And then — as the kiss went on and *on* — Bella felt Robert becoming more and more involved. More and more *passionate*.

When their kiss broke off, Bella was convinced that years had passed. That they had been married for half a century. That they had had dozens of grandchildren. A beautiful house in the countryside . . . her mother's house? Her heart ached to know what Robert himself must be thinking at that precise moment. It was a good thing that he apparently had no intention of leaving her in the dark with respect to that . . .

His eyes still fixed onto hers, and a light smile clinging to his lips, he said, "I can see a hole in your business plan — *several* holes, actually."

Bella took stock of what he was saying. At the romance — or pure *lack* thereof . . . It was only another second before she realised that she didn't care at all. In fact, wasn't it *more* passionate that he was taking an active interest in something that meant so much to her rather than trying to smother her with all that romantic nonsense other men gabbled out with seemingly no hesitation?

"Okay," Bella replied. "What are they?"

Robert smiled more widely, and then — before Bella knew exactly what was going on — he leaned into her once more, kissing her with greater force this time. He almost knocked her off her feet into the snow drifts surrounding them. When he drew back, he wore the same manic grin, the one which had — only minutes before — seemed impossible for him to conjure. "It would be better if we sat down. Went through them one by one. There's too many . . . I'm worried you might forget . . ."

"A date?"

Despite the kiss they had just shared, Bella couldn't help noting how Robert blushed fiercely. "Well, I . . . suppose you could call it that . . ."

But Bella wasn't going to let him get off so easily. She knew that words would do no use so she stepped into him and kissed him again. Before she knew it, they had their arms locked about one another. It was only when Woss started to bark that they finally broke off their embrace.

Realising that Woss was staring back off to the pub, Bella followed his stare. And saw that her mother, Adiema, Harriet and Dorothy had all emerged. And that — despite their obvious drunkenness — they were doing their best to treat this occasion reverently. It was only now, now that Bella and Robert had noticed them standing there, that they broke into feverish applause. It was then that Bella felt herself begin to blush just as Robert had done. As she reached down at her side for Robert's hand, felt his squeeze her own, she realised that she didn't really care if she was caught in a state of permablush for the rest of her life.

15

SWAMPED

Wearing his knee-high Wellington boots, Robert picked his way carefully across the sodden ground. Woss lagged at his heels, head bowed, reluctantly picking his way through Robert's footprints. The area was surrounded by sedentary diggers and other assorted construction machinery covered with weatherproof canvases. Work was due to start the next day. Robert had to admit, looking around the domain, to the forests which surrounded the otherwise featureless, and swampy terrain, that Lord Charles had his work cut out to create any sort of a resort in this place — let alone a *golf* course. Robert almost felt guilty about having taken Lord Charles on as a client now . . . and yet Lord Charles had been so insistent, he had been convinced that *Robert* should be the one to help him with his golf course pipedream, and when he had discovered that Robert had connections to Normonswold — his mother having lived the last period of her life here — that had only served to settle the matter once and for all in Lord Charles's mind.

There was a kind of eerie feel to the place.

The machinery which was yet to be switched on . . . the virgin land which had not yet been torn up. That realisation sent a twinge through Robert's gut, and then he reminded himself that he was an accountant, not a poet . . . like Bella.

Even as Robert found himself thinking about what she had written in the card which'd featured his mother's final home — Molinaar's Cottage — he wondered if only two words truly did constitute a poem:

To remember

That was all the card had said within.

And yet, they had somehow been exactly the right words — words which'd sent him sweeping back through the annals of memory. It'd brought him up against nostalgia; that old cloak and dagger.

He thought about the kiss they had shared on Christmas Eve. There had been something different about it. Something much . . . *deeper* than what he was accustomed to with his City Flings . . . did that *mean* anything?

And then he thought — unable to prevent himself from wincing — how he had been so nervous following the kiss that he had slipped into the only thing which made him feel comfortable: talking about business — *God, what an idiot!*

He tried to rescue the situation in his mind, reminding himself that Bella had wanted to clarify that the 'chat' he had in mind was in fact a 'date' . . . what'd he said? . . . 'I suppose you could call it that.'

What a cool customer he was.

How *impressed* Bella must've been by *that* display . . .

As he trudged on through the muck, feeling a steady drizzle beginning to fall, he thought about how Christmas Eve seemed such a long time ago now.

It'd been almost a month since their meeting.

Unfortunately, Robert had had to return to the city on Christmas Eve — just to pop into the office to tie up some bits and pieces. He was back in Normonswold for the first few weeks of construction. He was to be Lord Charles's 'eyes on the ground', to give him an impression of how everything was shaping up — not only on the construction site itself but how the good folks of Normonswold were dealing with the building works.

Robert was under no illusions. He knew Lord Charles wanted him to *spy* on Normonswold, to work out whether or not there might be any groups threatening to protest the plans for the golf resort.

Did Robert feel bad about this?

Well, to be quite honest, he felt conflicted.

On one hand, everything within him told him that what he had agreed to was deceptive — something not in tune with his personality at all . . . and then another something — and this was inarguably more powerful — told him it would be a Very Fine Thing Indeed to remain in close proximity to Bella.

As Robert made his way back to the car, he thought about how he could just drop by Molinaar's Cottage right now — right this moment . . . that would be a romantic gesture, wouldn't it?

Decided, he steered his attention onto where he had parked his car, and glanced back to gee Woss up for the final few yards back to the warm interior of the vehicle.

16

PANIC STATIONS

*B*ella listened to the phone ring and ring and ring against her ear. This was the sensation she had always dreaded, back when she had been working as a marketing professional. There seemed to be a different ring to the phone when someone was attempting to avoid your calls, and she was hearing it right now. She drew in a sharp breath then dropped the cordless phone down on the kitchen table, running her fingers through her hair, trying to get her mind straight on just exactly what this meant for Humble — what this meant for her *business*.

She knew it had been a mistake to make this deadline, for her to have made a distribution agreement with various retail outlets — and for them to pick up the first batch later on this afternoon.

It had been a day or two after Christmas, that was when Bella had felt that she was ready. That there was no point in waiting till the holiday was over. She was ready — Humble was ready — to start the New Year with a leaping stride. She had wanted to get cards into the stores before the end of January, and, well, she was about to blow that particular goal.

She was waiting on a printer, and had been for the past two weeks. She had made the order for the printer the same day she had agreed distribution with the retailers. And the manufacturers of the printer had informed her that the machine would be with her in a week or so's time. That 'week or so's time' had passed a good fortnight ago.

After chasing the machine every day, all too aware that today was the day that the distributor was dropping by to pick up the printed cards, she had finally got a call from the company which manufactured the machine telling her that it was out for delivery.

That it would be with her later that morning.

Well, it was now past noon and Bella was beginning to lose it.

The most frustrating thing was that the design templates were all set up and ready to go . . . all that was required was for them to hook up the machine, stock it with card and ink, and to press Print.

Bella constantly glanced up at the clock which hung from the kitchen wall, watching as five-minute blocks went by and as each did so picking up the phone another time and stubbornly jabbing out the number yet *again*. Only to be met with the never-ending ringing.

She did the sums in her head.

She had already memorised the operative capacity of the printer.

It could do two hundred and fifty cards an hour, although it was stressed in the literature that this was the maximum level of production. She had agreed to supply the retailers with a thousand cards, and she had until five o'clock that evening to print them. Even by her shaky arithmetic, she knew that if the machine didn't arrive by one p.m. then there simply wouldn't be enough time for her to get all the cards printed.

Not before the delivery lorry turned up.

She glanced at the clock, saw that it was now twenty-five minutes past twelve. She picked up the phone again, held it to her ear, and heard that constant ringing once more.

Someone knocked at the door.

Footsteps sounded in the house.

When Bella glanced up, she saw Cassandra appear in the kitchen doorway. She looked to Bella, and then to the front door. The two of them had been waiting for exactly the same thing. "I'll get it," Cassandra said.

Bella took a deep breath, set the phone down on the table, then gradually got to her feet. This was it . . . now she could *relax* . . . However, when she looked to the front hall, fully expecting to see a pair of men in overalls lugging an oversized cardboard box between the two of them, she had to admit that she was — at least momentarily — disappointed to see that it was Robert there, with Woss lagging at his heels, wagging his tail in a friendly, if slightly defeated manner. Bella could tell from the state of Robert's bright red cheeks, from the way that his hair was ragged and wild from the breeze, that the two of them had been out in the fields where Lord Charles intended to create his golf resort.

"Hi," Robert said, with a slightly coy smile.

"Hi," Bella replied, unable to keep herself from smiling back.

It was only when Cassandra emerged from the front hall, arms folded over her chest, that Bella was brought tumbling back to the present moment. Bella looked to Robert. "You didn't happen to see a lorry bumbling about the back lanes looking lost?"

Robert met her eye for a fraction of a second, then shook his head. He looked back at Cassandra, noting her firm look of concern, then turned to Bella once more. "This isn't a good time, is it?"

Bella explained — in impressively succinct and firm terms given the circumstances, she thought — just what the situation was.

Robert pouted momentarily then dug into the inside pocket of his overcoat. "What's the name of the manufacturer?"

"Why would you want to know?" Bella replied, only realising as she spoke the words, just how wound-up she sounded.

Robert, however, seemed unaffected by her tone — she supposed that as a City Accountant he was more than used to dealing with riled business people. "You'll see."

There being no reason not to, Bella gave Robert the name of the manufacturer, and Robert busied himself with his phone. There seemed to be no way that Robert had memorised the number for that particular manufacturer . . . but, then again, Bella supposed she didn't really know anything about Robert at all.

He was practically a stranger.

Robert gave Bella and Cassandra a knowing look and then — perhaps forgetting that this was no longer his mother's house — he wandered off in the direction of what was now Bella and Cassandra's studio. After precisely four minutes and seventeen seconds — Bella counted on the clock — Robert returned to the kitchen with a triumphant smile.

"Five minutes," he said.

Not knowing what else to do, Bella put the kettle on and soon enough each one of them had a cup of tea sat before them. There seemed to be nothing to talk about, so they all sat in silence, sipping at their warm drinks.

To begin with, Bella thought she was suffering from aural hallucinations, and then she was certain that she was feeling the beginnings of an earthquake. The truth, though, dawned on her soon enough. Her ears perked up and she set her mug down, no longer able to contain her accumulated nervous energy.

She dashed through the entrance hall and out through the front door. There — by some fairly robust miracle — was the delivery lorry, with the proverbial men dressed in overalls, lifting a large cardboard box off the back.

Rushing with a feverish high now, she almost wanted to help the men to lug the box in through the front door, to aid them in setting it down in the room she had allocated as being the *home* for the printer. But she relented.

She would hardly help matters by throwing her back out right now.

Feeling Robert and Cassandra's twin stare upon her and the delivery men as she escorted them through the kitchen, Bella oversaw the box's journey through the house to the designated room. When the men offered her the little machine to sign for the order, she was almost of a mind to get down on her knees and worship at their feet.

Perhaps she should be worshiping at Robert's feet.

With the delivery over and done with, the actual installation of the printer itself was remarkably painless. Bella had run through various nightmare fantasies about what precisely might happen during this process — everything from the printer refusing to switch on at all, to black smoke pouring from every orifice coupled with a nuclear-level explosion. Neither of these eventualities played out, however, and they had the printer up and running a little before one p.m. — it set off printing out the first batch of cards.

There was something unnerving about having to trust all her hopes and dreams to a machine doing its job correctly, but they had followed the manual to the letter — tending to the ink and card, and some other delicate operations — and all that was required now was for them to wait for the job to complete.

But waiting — *being patient* — wasn't among Bella's virtues.

Not today . . .

In the four hours that the printer went about its task, Bella estimated that she covered at least a half marathon in walking back and forth, up and down the corridor outside the room which housed the machine. Every fifteen minutes or so, she would allow herself to peer in at the tray which contained the printed cards.

Although she knew the machine was only capable of spewing out duplicates, she couldn't help but find herself eyeing up each one of the copies in the tray and wondering — *just wondering* — whether some aspect of Cassandra's illustration could be slightly improved, or if she really *should* have put *that comma there*, or *this exclamation mark here* . . . although Robert attempted to speak sense to her several times, she found it impossible to process his arguments. When he offered to leave and come back when she was through, and less busy, Bella had a rush of panic, something about not wanting to 'jinx' the printing process by changing any of the environmental conditions which'd been in place before it'd started.

It was hard to believe that the whole anxious process was over when the printer spat out the very last card of its run. When she glanced up at the clock, she saw that it had just gone five minutes past five. As if the whole world had stood still for Bella to appreciate this feat for just a second, there was another knock at the door, and — after hurrying the last run into the spare cardboard box they'd set aside earlier — she rushed through the house, opened the door and near enough *barked* at the delivery men to take the boxes of freshly printed cards away with them. It was only as she stood out on the street, staring at the back of the departing lorry that it struck her just what a big move this was.

That was it.

The first batch was gone.

There was no recalling the cards now . . . she had just gone and pushed a boat loaded with all her hopes and dreams out into the Real World. And she felt, well . . . kind of *numb*.

When she turned back to Molinaar's Cottage, she saw Robert and Cassandra standing on the doorstep — Woss sitting a little way inside the entrance, his head cocked to one side, patiently regarding her. She would have given a penny for his canine thoughts . . . she supposed that humans, when it really came down to it, were an exceptionally weird species.

Bella stood in the middle of the street for another few seconds before — with a well-earned shoulder-lifting-and-dropping sigh — she took a step back towards the house. And then she met eyes with Robert. "I had almost forgotten you'd come by to make good on our date — you haven't changed your mind, have you?"

Robert smiled back at her and shook his head.

When Bella looked to Cassandra, she saw that her eyebrows were raised. "And what about the champagne we've been keeping on ice for the first shipment?" Cassandra said. "A girl could get a little giddy drinking all that by herself."

Bella considered this. "All right," she said, "I think I've got a compromise."

The compromise which Bella struck was for them all to go back into the kitchen, and for them to take the champagne off ice. Since Bella hadn't got around to kitting the house out with champagne flutes so far, they had to make do with glass tumblers. She supposed that it was a good thing her mother wasn't hanging around to cluck her tongue with disapproval. The three of them raised their glasses and toasted Humble Greetings.

Bella noticed how Woss eyed them all curiously — clearly still trying to work out what was going on. Just what was so *special* about what had happened this evening.

Once they had all drunk their champagne, Bella's thoughts shifted back onto the matter at hand; namely her date with Robert. She looked at him, conscious of a slight smile curling the corner of her mouth. "Have you gone walking in the woods yet?"

" 'The woods' ? No, I can't say I have."

Bella glanced to Cassandra, who had an eyebrow arched and a grin firmly pressed onto her lips as she busied herself with washing up the glasses in the sink.

"Well, shall we go, then?"

Robert made to call Woss from where he had curled up in the corner of the kitchen to doze. But Bella held up her hand. "I'm sorry — if this is going to be a proper date then I believe it prudent to leave the children at home." She glanced again at Cassandra. "We should take advantage of having such a capable babysitter."

Cassandra stacked the washed-up tumblers on a tea towel, allowing them to drip dry. "Babysitter, old maid . . . I'm whatever you want me to be."

Robert hesitated a moment longer, clearly unsure about leaving Woss with Cassandra, but in the end — when Bella made to leave the kitchen — Robert followed without complaint.

17

WILDERNESS PASSIONS

$\mathcal{J}$t was about a fifteen-minute walk out of Normonswold to reach the woods, which were situated on the opposite side of the village from Lord Charles's proposed golf course.

The air was fresh, and there was the feeling of spring being just around the corner with the lighter evenings; the sun only now beginning to dip below the horizon. It was a good thing that Bella had had the foresight to bring along a pair of torches, which they soon clicked on to shine their way along the dark path.

Bella had to admit that spring had her apprehensive.

There was something about passing time which put pressure on her — the idea of deadlines still pushed her onwards, step by step, day after day, even though she had only herself to answer to now.

When Robert's hand subtly brushed her own, Bella's first reaction was to bat it away — almost as if her mind was too full to absorb any further input. A few minutes later, she succeeded in dragging herself back to the present moment. And she took the initiative. She reached out for Robert's hand, firmly entwining her fingers with his.

They clasped palms and walked on together, deeper into the woods.

Bella recalled back when she had been a child that her mother and father would always want to take walks in the woods, and how — after she'd reached nine or ten — she would do just about anything to get out of the excursions. She had never been the outdoors type. Perhaps that was how she had managed to not only put up with but *thrive* within City Life for such an extended period of time. Now, though ... over the past few months, actually ... she had grown to *appreciate* the passing seasons, the fauna and flora which surrounded Normonswold, in a way which she had never previously done so.

When she got down to it — when she analysed it the best she could — she believed it was because of the nature of what she was doing with her life now. She had soon decided that it would be one of the responsibilities of Humble to breathe in all the inspiration the real world had to offer, and then to neatly turn it into phrases and illustrations which could connect to the recipient ... or, better still, provide the link between the sender and recipient; saying something which was impossible to say under normal circumstances.

Humble Greetings was just as Bella had wanted it to be:

A facilitator for communication.

As they trod deeper and deeper into the woods, Bella became more and more confident about exactly where they were headed. She had had no concept of preplanning this trip — it was just the way that things had panned out.

They were headed for the cabin.

Although it was true Bella — and other girls and boys of a similar age — had similarly eschewed the woods whenever their parents had wanted to take them there, things had begun to change when they had hit fifteen or sixteen year.

That was when the woods suddenly became an incredibly attractive place.

Somewhere to get away from adults in such a small town. And the cabin was the centrepiece. As the shabby, decades-old wooden lodge came into sight around the corner, Bella felt a thrill pass through her stomach. There was a welcoming orange light lit on the porch. She could still recall the buzz of excitement which'd passed through her veins whenever she and a group of friends had decided to go down to the cabin, well stocked with beer, blankets, and whatever else they thought to take with them. If Bella had had more forethought — if she hadn't had such a manic day — then she might've remembered to bring along supplies.

As it was, though, they were empty handed.

But they had one another.

"Well, this place looks rather charming," Robert said, as they approached the cabin.

Bella saw, as she cast her gaze over the surroundings, that it was precisely as she recalled from over a decade ago. There was the still water of the pond around back, and — most important of all — the complete coverage of thick trees on the periphery of the clearing. It meant that nobody had a chance of stumbling across the spot. If anybody wanted to get to the cabin without a machete or a chainsaw, then they needed to come along this path, completely visible to the cabin occupants.

As they drew closer, and the porch light revealed more details to her, Bella couldn't help but see how the windows had been recently wiped clean. The porch area, too, had been swept of any leaves. As she surveyed the door, a plaque caught her eye:

The upkeep of this cabin, and the peaceable surrounding area, is dedicated to the memory of Swapan Drupada.

"Who's he?" Robert asked.

"I . . . don't know," Bella replied, which was the truth. She had no idea who he was. All she could say was that — at least from her recollection — she had never seen this plaque before. That meant it had only been put there in the past ten years.

She glanced back at Robert, reminding herself of where she was, of what they were doing. She raised a smile. "Whoever this is in memory of, they've certainly put their heart and soul into keeping this place clean and tidy."

"Shall we?" Robert asked, indicating the door with his open palm.

As if it would be any other way, the inside of the cabin was lovingly preserved. Although the space was simple, with twin camp beds, a small, round table, and a wood-burning stove, it was almost impossibly warm and cosy.

Once Bella had snapped on the light switch by the door, Robert approached the wood-burning stove, crouched down then said, "It's all stocked and ready to go." He rose back up. "Do you think we might be . . . I don't know . . . intruding on someone's romantic evening?"

It was then that Bella's eyes descended on the table. She realised there was an envelope there. There was no name or address written upon it. She trod over to it, took it up in her hands, and — trembling slightly — withdrew the folded note slipped inside:

Dear Guest,

I sincerely hope you are passing an enjoyable morning, afternoon, evening (please delete as appropriate) and I would like to welcome you to the cabin.

It is my intention that the cabin should be here always, for whoever might require it, a refuge out in the wilderness. It is with my time and attention that I maintain the cabin for these reasons, although, that said, there are a few housekeeping notes (I hesitate to call them 'rules' because nobody ever seems to follow rules). These are for dear guests to please leave the cabin in the state that they found it (which, if I do say it myself, is impeccable), and for said dear guests to please restock the wood-burning stove from the store around the back of the cabin when they leave.

You shall find blankets stowed away in the storage cupboards, as well as coffee, tea, bottles of fresh water, and an assortment of exotic wines and spirits for those who are 'of age'. A bathroom can be found through the solitary door — hot water is provided courtesy of a battery which is recharged constantly from the solar panels on the roof of the cabin.

Please enjoy your stay. I wish for the cabin to bring you as much joy and peace as it has me.

Yours faithfully,

The Humble Proprietor

" 'Humble' ?" Robert said, in an accusatory tone.

"Nothing to do with me."

The two of them stood in silence for the longest time, staring at the opened letter in Bella's hands. When Bella sensed the time was right, she folded the letter back up and replaced it within the envelope. And left the envelope right where she had found it.

"Do you suppose this place is meant for us?" Bella asked.

Even as she said the words, she wondered if she should explain further — but that didn't seem necessary. Robert understood precisely what she meant.

As he moved towards her, time seemed to slow.

His sapphire eyes locked onto her own.

He was a wild animal who had — at last — hunted her down.

And there would be no escape now.

His arms reached down and his hands clasped her firmly about the waist. Bella felt a shudder, although it had nothing to do with any draught which might've snuck its way into the cabin — no, the Proprietor had taken care of any such potential unpleasantries.

They stood like that for the longest time.

Gazes locked.

Sharing their warmth.

And then Robert's lips plunged downwards, onto hers. She felt his tongue trace the underside of her bottom lip. She quivered — all through her body. She felt Robert's muscles tighten, and his breaths shorten. Bella's heartbeat clanged in her ears like an unstoppable jungle rhythm. It drove her onwards — encouraged her to make the moves.

She reached up and combed her fingers through Robert's long, golden hair. It was so soft, and so smooth, and it felt like silk against her skin. She breathed him in — an earthy, elemental scent, seemingly made all the more intense by their surroundings.

He was like a wild animal returning home.

Their lips still locked together, Robert lifted Bella from the waist in a single movement, and he carried her the short distance over to one of the camp beds. As he prepared to let her drop, Bella had a nightmare vision of the camp bed folding up beneath her weight. When Robert did lay her down, she soon realised there was nothing to fear.

Slowly — *gently* — they shed their clothes. Each new centimetre of skin was a fresh discovery. It was hard to believe there was a world beyond the windows of the cabin when it seemed as if anything worth seeing in the universe was right here.

Right here in this room.

A conductor caught in the reverie of his orchestra, Robert drove them forwards, peeling back blankets, slipping them both beneath.

Here the warmth became almost overpowering.

Bella's head began to pound, but not with any sort of migraine — *no*, this was pure anticipation. *Excitement* for what was about to come.

Finally — *finally* — she felt him enter her. Their bodies pressed together. Their mouths fixed to one another. Their hearts tapping in time. She had to remind herself to breathe constantly. She was afraid that she was so happy in this moment — she was struck by such great pleasure — that she might just die right now. And she could little afford to die at this juncture in her life; not when she had just commenced her Life's Work.

The heat in the cabin rose and rose, and Bella felt their muscles press against one another. She felt their heartbeats rap harder and harder . . . coming closer and closer to a conclusion . . . to a time when all this would end.

Sinking her teeth into her bottom lip, Bella squeezed Robert's shoulders tightly, digging in her fingernails. She clung to him — never wanting this to end.

18

WALKING ON CLOUDS

When Bella returned to work, it felt as if she had been away for an entire month — rather than an evening and a morning. She was glad to find that Cassandra was taking care of the emails; and a little taken off guard when Cassandra showed her how they could track the shipment of cards they had sent out the day before. From the brief status report, Bella saw that the shipment was 'In Warehouse'.

"Any other news?" Bella asked.

"No," Cassandra replied, still staring at the computer screen. "Just me and Woss, sitting about, watching TV, finishing the champagne and chocolate, talking about how stupid love is and how it'll never happen to us."

"There was *chocolate*?"

Cassandra shrugged, a faint smile tracing her lips. "Doesn't matter now, does it?"

Not really knowing what to do with herself, Bella headed for the studio where she looked through Cassandra's most recent illustrations. She flipped through the drawings, a whole storm of potential words and phrases coming to her as if they were zapped directly into her brain from someplace out in the heavens. She supposed that one of the positive aspects of a reinvigorated sex life was an uptick in creativity.

However, whenever she sat down at her desk to write out her ideas, there was something off about the connection between the pen nib and the page. It seemed almost as if the page kept on sneaking its way out from beneath the pen — an incurable ink allergy. When the phone rang in the mid-afternoon, Bella was pleased to have an excuse to get up and away from her work. It was her mother. She wanted Bella to come round. Although her answer might've been different given other circumstances, she opted for the easy way out.

Cassandra was all too glad to come with her, and the two of them set out across the gusty landscape to Bella's mother's house.

It was Dorothy who answered the door — and it *was* Dorothy, not Kieran, given the long black dress he was wearing that day.

Dorothy escorted them through the house to the conservatory where Bella's mother was awaiting them, perched on her chair like a primed tiger, a teapot and cups artfully arranged before her.

From the smile on her mother's face, Bella couldn't help but wonder if news of her and Robert's exploits the night before had already travelled the length and breadth of Normonswold. That was one of the downsides of residing in such a small town — everybody knew everyone else's business . . . actually, that wasn't quite accurate; it was much more accurate to say that everybody was *living* in each other's business.

Bella tentatively took her seat, while Cassandra did the same. The two of them sensed the strained atmosphere, and neither one wanted to be the first to speak.

Right as Bella was certain that somebody was going to have to say *something*, she caught the divine scent of freshly baked goodies drifting into the conservatory. She turned in her seat and looked to the door, realising she could hear familiar voices.

Harriet and Adiema.

When they came into view, Bella watched as each of them bore a plate — Harriet with pleasantly bronzed scones, and Adiema with an assortment of pain au chocolat, croissants, and Danish rolls. It was now that Bella saw just what the remaining space on the table was going to be put to use for. Once the baked treats were on the table, Harriet and Adiema took their seats, while Bella's mother set about pouring tea for her guests. Her mother still wore an unreadable smile which was doing nothing but putting Bella more and more on edge.

"So wonderful that you could all join me here," Bella's mother said, pouring out a cup of tea for Cassandra. "I know how these things can be at such short notice — that it can be difficult to clear the time."

Bella took her chance and glanced about the faces of her mother's other guests, hoping she might be able to divine something of what was going on. But everybody looked just as confused as Bella herself felt.

"You will no doubt be wondering *why* I have called you here so urgently ..."

This was not phrased as a question, more as a statement that was intended to hang in the air and then drift away, as if tempting one of them to challenge it. They all knew Indigo Miles far too well to think that challenging her to *anything* was a good idea.

"Please," Bella's mother said, with an achingly sweet smile, "each of you take a pastry."

They all did as she said.

From the way they all withdrew their small plates bearing their goodies upon them, Bella wouldn't have thought it too far a leap of logic for someone looking through the window to think that her mother had just declared with glee that she had poisoned one of the baked goods. Nobody began on their treat. All eyes were fixed on Bella's mother — just how she liked it.

Bella's mother — *finally* — relented. "Lord Charles. *That* is the reason I have brought you all here today."

Perhaps it was testament to Bella's previous night of passion — and a glowing review of Robert's prowess — that it took her several moments to process exactly who Lord Charles was . . . and then it all came back to her, like a mouldy, soggy blanket.

"What about him?" Bella put in, before she could help herself.

She realised that this had been a somewhat rash judgement when she looked about Harriet, Adiema, Dorothy and Cassandra's faces, seeing that they were all staring at her, no doubt wishing to know just *why* she bore such a grudge against a man who had bought drinks for the whole town all Christmas Eve.

Bella's mother rested her tongue on her lower lip, as if judging her next line of action, whether or not she should try to get to the nub of what had caused Bella's sudden, heated reaction. In the end, though, she appeared to have a greater game in mind.

"It's his resort," Bella's mother continued. "Today is the first day of construction."

Another silence pressed down upon the group.

Then Adiema spoke up.

"But that's right, isn't it? I mean, he *did* say in all of the planning documents that he was going to start today . . ."

Bella's mother held her finger up for silence, shuttering her eyes to slits. "As I'm sure you are aware, the Normonswold Village Committee" — Bella was certainly *not* aware of such an organisation, and couldn't help wondering if her mother hadn't invented it on the spot, or if the Normonswold Village Committee represented nothing more than the end of the kitchen table which caught most sunlight — "has waged an elongated letter-writing campaign with Lord Charles, hoping to provoke a response to his proposals. It has not, however, received any such response from Lord Charles, or his team, and so now it is the Committee's opinion that action should be taken."

" 'Action' ?" Dorothy echoed. "What action?"

"*Action,*" Bella's mother continued, glowering at Dorothy with a needlelike stare, "to protect not only the wildlife and unique landscape surrounding Normonswold, but village life as we know and love it."

Bella didn't dare say anything. She could feel the tension in the air. She knew that when her mother got like this there was really nothing anybody could say or do to talk her down. It was with great reluctance that she decided to indulge her mother. "Has the Committee really received no response at all from Lord Charles?"

Her mother shifted her gaze onto Bella, and Bella felt an icy chill pass through — what she imagined to be — her soul. "The Committee has received no response of *substance* from Lord Charles . . ."

"So it *has* received a response," Harriet put in, taking her life into her own hands, or — perhaps more accurately — placing it into Bella's mother's.

Bella's mother glanced briefly at Harriet. "The Committee has received *several* replies from Lord Charles, in fact, but these *letters* all share the same tone and conclusion — that although our discomfort with his plans are unfortunate, there is simply nothing more that can be done. It is Lord Charles's opinion that he has already gone through all of the proper channels and acquired the appropriate permissions to go through with his propositions."

Yet another silence.

Bella couldn't help noticing that not one of them had yet touched their baked goods.

Her mother continued, "It is now the Committee's opinion that direct action is required."

"Sorry, Mum, what?" Bella said. " 'Direct action' ? What could that possibly mean?"

The tone of her mother's reply was that of an obnoxious child. "What do you *think* it means?"

"Protest?"

"Exactly."

The longest, most stunned silence yet followed.

Bella felt her heart beating hard against her ribcage. Even despite this situation — this *meeting* with what she took to be the entirety of the Normonswold Committee-cum-Dictatorship — she kept having flashbacks to the night before. To Robert's power. To his grace. To his *warmth* . . . the warmth they had shared into the early-morning light when he had had to go and get ready for work . . . when he had had to go and meet with Lord Charles at the site of his proposed golf resort.

Adiema cleared her throat and sat forward in her chair. "And what sort of protest might this be?"

"Well," Bella's mother replied, "to be quite honest with you, I thought that we might be able to do a little brain-storming on the subject."

The afternoon stretched on into the evening with Bella — and the other guests to a lesser degree — doing their best to dissuade Indigo Miles from her plans for 'direct action' against Lord Charles. Despite everything, though — despite the manic praise they each gave Bella's mother for her cooking and for her hosting of the impromptu afternoon tea — she remained entirely unmoved from her starting point. As they made their way out of the house, all of the guests headed for their own homes, and a well-deserved rest, Bella's mother stood at the front door, effectively cornering the whole lot of them.

"I want to know *when*," she said.

Bella didn't dare exchange glances with the others — that would've given away their group thoughts right away. Despite that, she knew that they were all waiting on her, that fairly or unfairly, they placed all the pressure upon Bella to 'deal' with her own mother . . . as if there was any adult child in existence who could truly exert any sort of control over their parents.

All the same, Bella decided — for the Greater Good — that she had to try.

"Mum," she began, in that all-too-familiar, childlike nasal tone, "I really don't think that this is a good idea — I think, perhaps, we should maybe try to have a meeting with Lord Charles, see if there isn't anything —"

Her mother waved this away at once. "No, no — the time for discussion has long passed. Lord *Charles*" — the way she said it was cloying — "has made it very clear that Normonswold represents nothing more than an irritable splinter in the sole of his foot. He wants nothing further to do with the village or the people who live here just as long as he can get exactly what he wants."

Bella suppressed the urge to tear her hair out over the fact that her mother understood exactly what was going on — how she had grasped the exact subtleties of the situation, and yet refused to accept this as a satisfactory answer.

"Mum," Bella started again and reached out for her mother's arm.

Her mother was quick, though — clearly wily when it came to heavy-handed mother-daughter interaction. She ducked out of the way of Bella's grasp and met Bella's gaze with a renewed fury in her eyes. "You listen to *me*, Bella. You may think that Normonswold means nothing since you moved away from here, but it's your home again now. Just as it's *my* home — *our* home . . . are we going to allow this . . . this *revolting* man place a stake in the ground so near to where we rest our heads at night?"

Bella frowned, unsure quite what to make of this development.

Her mother continued to meet her gaze for another moment or so, and then relented.

This proved the signal for Dorothy — speaking for the whole group — to announce their exit afresh. This time, when Dorothy led Adiema, Harriet and Cassandra to the door, Bella's mother didn't stand in their way. In fact, Bella's mother opened the door and then stood back to allow them through.

Although it required great strength not to follow Cassandra out of the house and back to the refuge of Molinaar's Cottage, Bella knew that it was her daughterly responsibility to get to the bottom of this. And so she stood firm.

When Bella was content that the departing footsteps had crunched their way sufficiently up the driveway, so that there was no chance of her or her mother being heard, Bella turned to her. "Is there something you want to tell me, Mum?"

There was a moment's resilience.

Then a firm-eyed glare.

And — all at once — her mother was broken.

19

SHATTERED SILENCE

*B*ella guided her mother back into the kitchen, got her sat down at the table, and — as always whenever there was Serious Work to be done — she put on the kettle.

Once the kettle had boiled, and the two of them had a steaming cup of tea sitting before them, Bella did her best to cut to the quick. She asked her mother straight out just what her history with Lord Charles was.

"It's not a particularly bright story, Bella, but . . . hopefully you will be able to understand — and be able to understand my thought process from it."

Bella sipped at her tea, never taking her eyes off her mother, as if she might evaporate into thin air if she lost concentration for even a moment.

"I first met Charles Knightly" — Bella noticed how she dropped Lord Charles's title — "several years ago. *Decades* ago, actually. It was while I was still together, with your father, before we had had you."

To Bella, there was always something deeply strange about considering the idea that her parents had lives before she was born. Of course, it was obvious and logical, and yet — when she really thought it through — it was deeply odd to think that she had been shaken out of oblivion and fallen into their lives.

"It was soon after we married — soon after we moved in here, to *Ebbendevor* — that I was acquainted with Charles Knightly for the first time. He was younger then, obviously, a lot trimmer than he is these days. But he was — and still is — the same person."

Bella held herself still, her hands wrapped about her mug, feeling the absorbed warmth radiating through her bloodstream.

Bella's mother shut her eyes for such a long time that Bella was convinced tears would commence to snake down her cheeks. But the tears didn't come. Bella took this as a sign of resilience — that her mother wouldn't *cry* for Charles Knightly . . . not for *him*.

"He came to our door, 'just in the neighbourhood', as he put it. Your father was at work upstairs while I had been tending to the kitchen — keeping it tidy. When I first set eyes on him, I had no thought about making excuses. I had nothing but time. I had taken care of all the morning chores. I think, back then, I even *thought*, with your father beavering away upstairs, hard at work, that it was somewhat *pleasant* to have this gentleman caller to break up the mundanity of the day. I even had the glimmer of the idea that it might make your father, uh . . . *jealous* in some way . . . that it might reignite a passion in him which I was already beginning to suspect was starting to fade." Her mother swallowed hard then glanced down at her clasped hands. "So, I invited him in, asked him if he would like a cup of tea, and then I took to showing him the grounds. He was so *interested* in *Ebbendevor*, in all the old stories, you know, and it was such a nice thing to be able to actually *talk* to someone at that time. Although I'd grown up in the house, there had always been my brothers and sisters, my mother and father, to speak with. When your father and I began living there alone, I never thought that I would ever feel *lonely*."

Feeling a pounding at her temples — a migraine likely coming on — Bella drew in a deep breath then focused in on her mother once again.

"It was on the way back into the kitchen that he first touched me. It was very subtle. He merely laid his palm in the small of my back, as if supporting my balance as I made my way up the steps, returning to the kitchen. When I felt his grip becoming firmer, I made a quiet allusion to my husband upstairs, working. That seemed to throw him out completely. At least his hands didn't become any busier than they had been moments' before. Soon after, he made his excuses and left . . . I was alone again in the house."

"And then what happened, Mum?"

"Oh, he never called around at the house again; that would have been far too . . . *scandalous* . . . but I would see him around Normonswold. Goodness knows why, but he's always seemed to have his eye on this place. The villagers, though, seem to have short memories, or perhaps it's just the fact that I'm the only one who remembers when he was buzzing around here before."

Bella's mother stopped, and Bella was unsure whether or not she should push her to continue. In the end, her mother went on of her own accord.

"To tell the truth, I never really exerted much thought on Knightly. And his appearances in Normonswold became less frequent, until he seemed to grow tired of the place. If only."

Her mother's voice was tighter now, and her focus had narrowed, as if she had targeted a specific memory and — no matter how slippery, how elusive — she was going to pin it down.

"It was a Saturday when I'd gone out to see your Aunt Pollyanna. I had taken the car, leaving your father at home, to his 'work'."

Even now, even after all these years, Bella sensed the resentment in her mother's voice for how her father had made her feel so lonely . . . so *unloved*.

"It was getting dark by the time I made my way back through the country lanes, headed for Normonswold, and *Ebbendevor*. I've never been the most confident driver, and it was the time of year when the fog had begun to draw in, so I was already feeling somewhat nervy. You can imagine how I felt when a car began to trail me, when — in the rear-view mirror — headlights began to dazzle me. I can still recall how I felt this creeping, tingling sense all over the surface of my skin. I started to tremble. And there was nothing for me to do except pull over at the side of the road and to allow the car to pass me. But when I did pull into the side of the road, the car behind did the same. I thought about what I should do, if I should take off again into the fog, but I was frozen. And then . . . and then . . . I saw *his* face in the rear-view mirror."

Acting on instinct, Bella reached across the table and took hold of her mother's hand. Just as her mother had been telling in the story, Bella felt her mother shaking now. It was as if a sudden chill had crept into the room. Well, she supposed that Lord Charles *was* an exceptionally unpleasant chill . . .

"He . . . he . . . asked if I was okay . . . when I saw his smile I felt so . . . so reassured. Like everything would be . . . *fine* from now on." Her mother snorted hard, trembled still harder, but somehow managed to hold herself together. "He asked me . . . asked me if I wanted to get into his car, with him . . . he said that he would drive me back home . . . and I . . . well, I . . . I *believed* him."

Bella squeezed her mother's hand.

And her mother — albeit faintly — squeezed back.

"I don't really remember . . . I don't really . . . . really remember exactly what happened . . . just wanting to get away . . . it all happened so quickly . . . I was so . . . so *numb* . . . and yet when . . . when it was over, I recall thinking to myself that . . . that I could go home . . . that it was time for me to *go home* now."

An all-consuming silence swallowed the kitchen whole.

Bella felt a tingle — perhaps the same tingle her mother had felt — shudder across the surface of her skin. Every muscle in her body tautened. But she needed to be strong. She couldn't lose control. Not now. Not while her mother needed her.

"I never said anything to your father — nothing to *anyone* — I'm . . . I've never really known how to describe what . . . what happened . . . in a way, it was like a dream, like a nightmare, something about it wasn't real." It was now that Bella's mother raised her gaze, that she pressed her lips tightly together. "He's not your father, Bella, I can reassure you of that much."

Bella felt as if the air had grown arid and thick, and that it pressed in on her eardrums, kneading her brain within her skull. "Why did you want to go — on Christmas Eve? Why did you accept all of those free drinks Lord Charles was offering?"

Bella's mother remained still for the longest time again. Bella was brought in mind of a baby bird, yet to grow feathers — yet to gain the ability of flight. Unable to escape.

"I wanted to . . . test myself . . . and, I suppose, to test *him*." Bella's mother smiled grimly. "He didn't recognise me after all these years. It seems that I have transformed beyond all measure." She gazed long and hard at Bella. "I saw how he treated you, though, and it showed me better than any single scrap of evidence that he is the same man — just a few years older. You can't believe how happy it made me feel to see you and Robert together at the end of that night, and to see that *he* was out of the picture."

Bella felt herself blush slightly to hear her mother speak of Robert by his name. She reminded herself that she wasn't sixteen any longer, but it didn't seem to help. There was something about Robert which brought out her inner sixteen-year-old.

There was a long silence in the kitchen before Bella's mother made eye contact again. "What do you say about driving this lecherous old man out of town?"

It felt as if it was the first time in months that Bella's mind wasn't completely occupied with thoughts of Humble. She held her mother's stare, then smiled slightly. "I always did fancy being part of a riot."

2 0

RESISTANCE

*T*he early-spring sunshine streamed over the whole of the construction site as Robert squelched his way through the soppy mud in his Wellington boots.

There was a cacophony of shouted commands, bleeping machines, and various frequencies of grinding engines.

Robert had been to his share of construction sites and he would have been happy to declare that this one was one-hundred-percent in keeping with his expectations. Lord Charles would be happy to hear that everything was going Very Smoothly Indeed.

As Robert picked his way past an excavator, digging a large hole for what reason Robert really had no idea, he felt a twang of discomfort in his stomach for having to leave Woss in the car. He could still recall the barely restrained delight in Woss's eyes as they had pulled up here, and then the mountainous disappointment when Robert had barked at him to *Stay*. That said, a building site was no place for a dog. Robert caught himself wondering whether or not he should've asked Bella to look after Woss throughout the day. Since she was at Molinaar's Cottage, with a garden, and had far more space to run around than the foot well of a passenger seat, it would've been a much better option.

But Robert hadn't wanted to presume.

It was all very well what was going on between them, but he didn't want to start treating her as if she would rush to perform any favour he asked . . . even if she was willing.

Robert felt the warmth on his cheeks and he undid his overcoat a few buttons, preparing to go and meet with the foreman in his canvas tent erected near the field gate. He was aware that the dumper truck had been running late that morning — the foreman had asked Robert to chase this, but when he had tried to get them on the phone it had just rung and rung. The dumper truck operators would be in for an earful when they did finally turn up — nobody ignored Robert Rutherford's calls and got away with it . . .

As Robert made his way over to the tent, with the thought of perhaps asking Bella out to Old Couple's Café later that afternoon, he was struck by a bizarre sight. He paced more quickly, his heartbeat increasing. He could see the foreman running down the road . . . that he was in a panic about something. Robert broke into a jog — as fast as he dared go given the soft ground underfoot.

When he passed through the gate, and emerged onto the road, he saw that several contractors were standing and watching what was taking place.

What *was* taking place?

Robert's mind slowly made sense of the group of six women — wait, were they *all* women, or was one a man dressed in women's clothing? — who, each bearing a sign, were blocking the road so that the recently arrived dumper truck could make no further progress towards the field without running one or all of them down.

As he came closer to them, his focus became sharper, and he recognised one face above all others among them.

Bella.

What was she *doing?*

As Robert marched up to the group of would-be protestors, he saw that the foreman had already gone red in the face, caught in a shouting match with the lady who Robert recognised to be Bella's mother. Was there any way this could've been *more* awkward?

"Clive? Clive?" Robert said, addressing the foreman.

The foreman — Clive — broke off from his remonstrations, turning to look at Robert. Although he was red in the face and clearly committed to this argument, he appeared glad for Robert to step in.

"I'll see you back at the tent," Robert said.

Clive nodded then turned back for the field, shaking his head. "All right."

Robert shot a cursory glance at the dumper truck, and the operator who was still sitting behind the wheel, revving the engine. Robert acted quickly, instructing the operator to switch off the engine and to get down from the cab, although it seemed to be the equivalent of asking Samson to have a haircut.

That done, the operator standing rather sheepishly beside the cab of the truck, ready to hop back up the steps at a moment's notice, Robert turned his attention to the group of protestors. Bella's mother still stood at the front of the group, and Robert did his best not to pin on a professional smile — he always liked to meet these potentially explosive situations head-on, in a sincere manner . . . not like some salesperson or customer service representative . . .

"How are you all today?" Robert asked.

Bella's mother didn't shift from the spot — wasn't her name Indigo . . . Indigo Miles?

Indigo Miles stared him down. Even if she did know about him and her daughter it didn't seem that this was going to help him out of the conflict. "We would be a lot better if Charles *Knightly* picked up his mess and got out of town."

Robert was shocked by the sharp tone of her response. He thought back to the not-entirely-successful Christmas Eve at the Thicket Arms. He had not missed the fact that there was a steady stream of resentment bubbling just below the surface within most villagers — just that it had slipped his mind a little given what had happened later on . . . the *card* which Bella had given him . . . *that kiss* . . . the night at the cabin.

In a way he had been expecting something of this order, even if Lord Charles had been adamant that he was being overly cautious. Lord Charles had truly believed that because he had bought them a few drinks, he had the villagers eating out of the palm of his hand.

"Mrs Miles," Robert began, already feeling that he was allowing a slight tremor to enter his tone of voice — he thought it might be because Bella was there, watching on with the rest of them. "You are perfectly right in what you are doing, and there is no way we can compel you to allow the truck through to the construction site. Would you please let me know if there is anything I can do for any of you? We have hot drinks. Coffee? Tea?"

Behind Indigo, Robert saw several of the women's eyes light up. The sun was shining but the trees along the road cast them in shadow so he supposed they were a little chilly. Indigo, however, met Robert's eye and shook her head sternly. "Our terms are very plain, Mr Rutherford. I know that you only have permission for vehicles to enter the site between the hours of eight in the morning and six at night. We shall not allow so much as *one* onto the site between those hours, though any vehicle which wishes to leave is more than welcome to do so . . . that said, getting back onto the site might prove problematic."

Robert felt his stomach churn slightly. He hadn't missed the fact that she had entirely sidestepped his attempt at diplomacy. But that didn't mean he didn't have a few more tricks up his sleeve. "I'll tell you what," Robert said, "I can get in touch with Lord Charles and ask him to meet with you to discuss your concerns —"

"We're not leaving this spot, no matter what *conditions* you lay out."

When Robert glanced up, he expected to see some of the other women with Indigo beginning to get itchy feet, but, surprisingly, they all seemed just as driven as Indigo herself. He shifted his attention back to Indigo. "I wouldn't imagine that you would leave this spot, only that I can arrange for a conversation between your group —"

"The Normonswold Village Committee."

"— and Lord Charles."

Robert knew that now would be the traditional time in negotiations to walk away from the table — to give the other side time to think about just what was on offer. But — and perhaps it was because Bella was with them — he just couldn't face the prospect of turning his back and walking away so coldly.

Indigo remained resilient, however. "There's no conversation to be had, *Robert*."

Hearing his first name spoken in those terms sent a shiver through his guts. He tried not to pay too much attention to the sensation.

"Your mother would be *ashamed* if she knew what you were doing."

This was the first time that Robert felt himself truly losing ground in the discussion. He floundered, internally, trying to think of a way back up into a commanding position. "She always loved Normonswold, which is why she would have wanted its financial future to be assured. For her grandchildren," he added, without really thinking it through, accidently making eye contact with Bella, and beginning to blush.

"Your *mother*," Indigo continued, "would have stopped at nothing to keep a lecherous beast such as *Knightly* out of Normonswold."

"This isn't about the . . . environmental impact, then?" Robert asked, wanting to bleed as much information from this increasingly uncomfortable conversation as he could manage.

"No, it's about the *man*."

Robert looked to the group of women, and then glanced to the dumper truck — the operator who had now pulled out his mobile phone and was tapping away at the screen. He sucked in a final lungful of air knowing that his only chance now was to push his luck.

It was a challenge in itself to keep his tone of voice level.

"As I have already offered, I can arrange for a personal meeting with Lord Charles. He would be only too happy to discuss your concerns. Failing that, you are most welcome to protest here, and to prevent as many vehicles from gaining access to the site as you please. As for Lord Charles's profile" — even as he spoke the words, he felt like he was making a mistake just from having engaged on this level — "I can only reaffirm that he is a man of good standing, well-respected, and with the community's best interests at heart . . ." When he saw a tear roll down Bella's cheek, he lost the thread of what he was saying.

Open-mouthed, wanting more than anything to go and console

her, he expected nothing less than for Indigo Miles to smell blood and to move in for the kill.

Instead, though, she turned her attention to her daughter.

Robert was stuck for several moments, caught between business and leisure, and unsure exactly which one he should be prioritising at that particular time.

In the end, Indigo made up Robert's mind for him.

She called the other protesters together and they moved out of the road. Before they set off back in the direction of the village, Indigo turned to look at Robert for a final time.

"Feel free to come and go as you please today, but tomorrow we will be back, and with greater numbers. There is no discussion to be had . . . Knightly will not be successful with his endeavour, I can assure you that, and what's more, anyone who aids or abets him will only be standing in our way. An *enemy.*"

As Indigo led Bella away from him, Robert felt as if his whole body might split apart . . . but there was nothing he could do.

He watched the group out of sight, and then found himself meeting the dumper truck operator's eye. The operator had broken into a grin. He slipped his mobile phone away, got down from the cab and patted Robert on the shoulder. "Good job, pal. *Women,* eh?"

Robert continued to look off along the road, in the direction in which the group had disappeared. ". . . Yeah," he replied, dryly.

21

TIME AND TEARS

*B*ella found it difficult to control herself as she lay face down on her bed in Molinaar's Cottage, the tears dampening her pillow. She could hear her heart beating hard in her ears, and feel the sensation of her breathing ploughing through her. She wanted to get away — she wanted to go back to her old life. Sure, there had been issues with the Big City, but weren't they better than being stuck in some bumpkin town where she would never truly be able to escape *anybody*? Just how anybody managed to live out their entire life here without feeling the need to blow their head off somewhat escaped her.

There was a knock at her bedroom door.

Bella said nothing.

She wondered if she just lay very still — and cut out the sniffling — anybody would even know she was here.

The door opened.

As Bella tracked the footsteps across her bedroom, she was certain that it would be Cassandra's voice she would hear. As it turned out, however, it was not Cassandra at all. When the person did speak, she instantly recognised that it was Harriet.

Harriet? . . . What was she doing here?

"Bella," Harriet said, speaking Bella's name impossibly lightly, "it's going to get better. What we're doing, it's for the best of the village. We have a duty to stick together — to stick up for one another. Normonswold is one big family, you have to recognise that."

Bella couldn't help but feel herself swept back to her previous life, to when she had used such words as 'family' and phrases like 'stick together' as empty signals to the potential customer . . . hoping to strike them on some elemental level.

Well, Harriet had certainly struck her on an 'elemental' level now.

It was then that Bella felt Harriet's palm flat between her shoulder blades, gently rubbing her back. There was something about the touch which sent waves of warmth through her entire body. It was a deeply relaxing sensation — something which allowed her to cut her mind free from the otherwise nonstop rush of thoughts which bombarded it.

She pictured a still, pristine sea, and a crystal-clear horizon, a gentle, warm breeze against her cheeks.

Bella's heartrate slowed still further.

Her breaths came deeper.

And then, before she really knew what was happening, she drifted off into a doze.

When Bella came to, it was dark in her bedroom.

She was not entirely unaccustomed to this. Sometimes, when

137

she and Cassandra had been going at some particular aspect of Humble all night and most of the morning, she would tumble into bed after midday, waking up just before dinner, before returning to work. Now she understood why trendy corporations encouraged employees to take naps at work . . . it was certainly a good way of refreshing the mind, of keeping yourself going at the job in hand without going home — the only difference was that Bella was already home.

Bella shifted out from beneath her duvet, feeling a draught around her shins. She slipped the dressing gown hanging off the door over her t-shirt and jeans. As she made her way out of the bedroom, she realised she could hear voices in the kitchen. When she made her way out, along the hall, they got so loud that Bella could only assume that there was a flaming argument at hand. She only made it halfway down the stairs when she caught her mother's voice rising above them all, calling them to order.

She flirted with the idea of returning to bed and pretending that she hadn't heard anything. This reminded her all too clearly of when she was a little girl and her parents would argue and how she would tiptoe about the house, praying that they wouldn't hear her footsteps, lest they turn their ire onto her. Before Bella had fully got through considering an escape plan, however, she was spotted — from the bottom of the stairs — by Cassandra. It was more out of desperation than anything that Cassandra gestured for Bella to come down and join her. Bella performed her bidding, the two girls heading into the kitchen where heated battle was taking place.

The first thing Bella noticed was Woss pressed up against the wall opposite her, eyes cocked backwards, eyes wide, staring at everyone with canine disbelief.

Then Bella took stock of the details, of the scene itself.

Her mother, standing with her hands on her hips. Adiema in a similar pose, at Bella's mother's shoulder, Harriet lingering a few steps behind but with no less of a fierce expression pressed onto her face. Then — of course — there was Robert.

Bella's heart skipped a beat to look at his face.

He glanced briefly at her, before returning to Bella's mother.

Bella couldn't help but feel a touch of disappointment. He had looked at her as if she was a stranger, as if the two of them had never met, as if the night in the cabin had never even happened. Bella felt herself harden inside. She wasn't going to burst into tears this time — this time she would be stronger.

Bella's mother arched her back as she shrieked at Robert, a scolding finger outstretched, flexing and unflexing as appropriate. ". . . It's *just* like I said back at the site — we're not interested in being fobbed off with excuses. We want nothing but for Knightly to get the hell *out* of Normonswold."

Despite her mother's tone, Bella saw that Robert was as unflustered as ever. He stood with his arms down by his side, palms resting lightly on his thighs. Today his hair looked a touch unkempt, as if he hadn't quite had the time to give it his usual attention with a brush.

"That is exactly what Lord Charles wishes to discuss, if you would just sit down . . ."

But Bella's mother was shaking her head all over again. "I'm afraid that we're speaking different languages. Perhaps I should make this easier for you, Robin —"

"Robert."

"— Robert," Bella's mother corrected herself, although Bella knew that using the wrong name had been nothing but intentional, a perfect method of antagonising a foe, "what we're asking for is simple, though it might not be *easy* to accomplish. In short, we want an official letter from Knightly declaring and outlining — in the most legal way — his planned withdrawal from Normonswold. Does that sound reasonable?"

When Bella read Robert's features, she knew that he could have no reply but to say that this was *entirely* unreasonable. However there was no way that Robert could say that and maintain any sort of standing in the conversation — he had to work out another way.

It was then that Robert caught her eye.

Bella knew that if she wished to be faithful to her mother, and the Cause, she should avert his gaze. And yet she found it impossible. It surprised her somewhat when Robert spoke to her. She had believed his thoughts were fully focused on her mother, and the blazing row which was playing out in the kitchen.

"Bella? Are you up to anything this evening?"

Bella glanced to her mother, seeing that she had opened her mouth to respond, clearly believing that Robert wouldn't *dare* have the nerve not to reply to her ultimatum. And although her mother's expression remained opened-mouthed and disbelieving, she didn't actually say anything. Bella shifted her attention back to Robert. "No, no plans."

"Would you like to go for a walk?"

At the word 'walk', Bella couldn't help noticing Woss's ears pricking up in anticipation. She shifted her attention back onto Robert. "Okay," she replied, and then, before her mother or anybody else could say anything, she rushed off into the hall and grabbed her coat.

Before she knew it, the two of them were outside — walking hand in hand — in the fresh night-time air.

"Your mother is certainly a *fierce* woman," Robert said.

"She's quite stubborn when she gets her mind around something." It was only now, about five minutes from Molinaar's Cottage, that Bella felt a scrap of remorse — as if she might indeed be betraying her mother, if not the Cause, by having stepped out with the Enemy. Her mother and the others had consoled her earlier on, after all. And although the thought crossed her mind that Robert might be using this meeting to gather information to feed back to Lord Charles, so that he might have a running chance at winning over the hearts and minds of the Normonslanders, Bella knew that it was just paranoid.

She and Robert were merely stuck in some silly game.

It would all play out soon enough, wouldn't it?

Woss sniffed along the path ahead of them. His tail stuck up proudly to the sky as he trotted over the damp ground. The two of them just watched Woss for a while, neither one of them apparently having anything to say.

"I have to tell you something, Bella," Robert said, as they turned the corner.

"Is it about work?"

"Uh, no ... not really."

"Okay, go on then."

Robert gently allowed his fingers to drift free of Bella's. He stopped walking and turned to face her. "Are you planning to spend the rest of your life in Normonswold?"

Bella felt as if she had been struck in the solar plexus. She was winded by the question for a long few moments. Then she said, "I don't know."

Robert met her eye, then nodded to himself. "Okay," he replied, then bowed his head, took her hand again, and they carried on, in Woss's wake.

When they inevitably returned to Molinaar's Cottage, Bella guessed that the time had to be around half past ten at night. She half expected to return to an utterly silent house, for only Cassandra to be up at the kitchen table, a freshly made cup of hot chocolate steaming away before her — perhaps sketching some detail which'd caught her eye in a magazine, or else reading a book. It *was* certainly quiet at Molinaar's Cottage, but Bella was somewhat put out to see that her mother hadn't yet taken her leave. Though neither had Adiema or Harriet. The only person missing — come to think of it — was Dorothy.

Although Robert exercised forceful control with everything he did, Bella couldn't help but overhear his sharp intake of breath as he realised that the day's arguments weren't yet over. However, apparently sensing tension brewing again, Bella's mother was quick to rise to her feet and to show Robert open palms, as if in surrender. "I wanted to invite you around my home one day," she said.

Bella didn't get the chance to sneak a glance at Robert, but she couldn't help but imagine a look of open-mouthed shock stretched over his face.

"Okay," Robert replied.

Nodding, as if to convince herself that this was the right idea, Bella's mother continued, "Sunday lunch sound good?"

Robert met her eye. "Do you want Lord Charles to attend —"

He had hardly got the words out before Bella's mother was shaking her head, as if to dissipate the very soundwaves he had caused by speaking. "No, just you — you are the only person who's invited. Well" — she paused briefly — "other than the rest of the Normonswold Village Committee."

Robert glanced around the kitchen, and Bella found it nigh-on impossible to read him. She knew that he would be confused, despite his ice-cold nature . . . he would be rendered confused by the sudden change in Bella's mother's attitude to him.

"Thank you," Robert finally got out.

"See you on Sunday, then," Bella's mother said.

There was an uncomfortable moment where nobody seemed to be heading for the front door, and it was only after several beats that Robert realised Bella's mother was *expecting* him to take his leave then and there. Bella reached down and squeezed Robert's hand out of sight, silently cutting him free for the time being — allowing him to escape the pressure cooker.

22

THE ANXIOUS HOSTESS

*F*ollowing her mother's instructions, Bella turned up at *Ebbendevor* just after nine o'clock in the morning. She had decided to go with a prim, cheerful yellow dress, with a pair of practical, light-brown tights for the sneaky chill which was still hanging over Normonswold. There was a bizarre moment where Bella's mother greeted her on the doorstep with a distant look in her eye, as if Bella was seeing her mother's resolve softening in the face of what was to come. It wasn't often Bella got the chance to see a genuine chink in her mother's armour.

It was hard to believe the activity when Bella stepped over the threshold of the kitchen, seeing steam billowing forth from seemingly countless pots and pans. The smells, too, were delicious. They sent trembles through Bella's stomach. Unsure exactly what she could do, Bella just hovered about in the middle of the kitchen until her mother snapped out of her daze and got her busy chopping carrots.

At nearly midday, Bella surfaced from the toil she was putting into her mother's lunch. She blinked away her daze, clearing her thoughts. She had almost forgotten — in all the preparation — that Robert was coming. When she heard the knock at the door, she almost leaped right out of her skin. It was only as she passed through the house that she caught sight of herself in several mirrors, and wondered if she shouldn't duck quickly into the nearest toilet to sort herself out somewhat . . . but another insistent knock at the door told her that there was no time for inefficiencies like making herself pretty. She opened the front door. And she saw right away that it wasn't Robert who was there.

It was Lord Charles Knightly.

Bella was so shocked to see the man there that she lost the ability to speak for several moments. She just stared at his pudgy crimson cheeks, unable to get a word out. Then, without any more time to set herself straight, Lord Charles leaned in through the doorframe, planting a kiss on each of her cheeks, and pinching her bottom as he did so.

Thankfully this particular physical interaction with Lord Charles was mercifully brief.

She was soon looking Lord Charles's assistant — George? — in the eyes.

Although she couldn't be certain, Bella thought she saw some note of apology in his expression. As if he acknowledged and understood the monster who was his boss . . . but still he did *nothing* . . .

Bella casually noted to herself how Lord Charles bore a bottle of champagne with a ribbon tied about its neck, as well as a mysterious, wrapped box. At least he had had the good manners to bring a gift with him . . . that was the very least he could've done.

Once the two men had entered the house, Bella had the strong thought that she should go and warn her mother in the kitchen, but that was when she heard more voices, and saw that the entire Normonswold Village Committee — as promised — was steadily crunching its way up the driveway, making steady progress towards the house. When they reached the front step, they all greeted Bella one by one — Adiema, Harriet, Dorothy and Cassandra . . . although Cassandra was clearly not an *official* member of the Committee, Bella had supposed that she was invited too; at least she would be more invited than Lord Charles and his crony . . .

Bella told the others they could find her mother in the kitchen, satisfying herself that her mother would be safe with the soon-to-arrive chaperones — and, anyway, hadn't her mother told her that Lord Charles hadn't recognised her at all when they had met at the pub? Then again, perhaps the surroundings here would have the effect of jogging his memory. Bella could only hope that this would all come to an end today.

That the past would be put to rest.

Otherwise . . . well, the alternative was unbearable to even consider.

Bella closed the door and waited patiently inside the front hall for Robert. She didn't want him to see her too eager, some young girl sat on the steps, kneecaps pressed together, waiting for him to arrive. When she finally did hear the car, she didn't allow herself to open the door right away. She stood and waited, head slightly bowed, listening to the car door slamming, then the light-padded footsteps and occasional snorts of Woss accompanying his owner up to the house. When Robert knocked, Bella waited the longest time before answering. She listened to him — on the other side of the door — breathing so gently, so evenly. There was a patience in his breathing which told her that he would wait all day if he had to ... and her mother had gone and picked a fight with him ...

When Bella opened the door, she immediately searched out his honey-coloured eyes.

They locked onto hers.

Before she could say anything, they fell into one another, Robert's lips locking onto hers. She felt his heart beating against her ribcage. His fingers combed her hair. His lips were so soft, and his skin was so smooth ... Bella knew that she could lose herself forever in Robert, if that was what she wanted.

An enormous clatter brought Bella back to the present.

She pushed herself away from Robert's chest because it seemed that the only way to break the magnetic attraction which drew them together was by pure force.

Still startled, and still mentally with her lips pressed tightly up against Robert's, she bounded in the direction of the kitchen. When she rounded the doorway, she immediately saw the culprit. One of the saucepans — and its watery contents — lay on the tiles at their feet. There was an almost perfect silence as none of the invitees said anything. The only sound was the bubble of the other saucepans on the stove.

In the end, it was Dorothy who spoke first. "Well, there goes lunch."

Thankfully for all involved, the damage wasn't too dramatic, although the scene which had followed hadn't been anything short of bizarre. To see the Normonswold Village Committee with Lord Charles and his assistant standing idly by, in shock, had been something she hadn't so much as *considered* seeing today. With

Lord Charles's arrival, however, everything was inextricably changed.

All the same, despite Lord Charles's presence there, Bella's mother went about her business as usual, returning to her affable manner, and urging them all to take their seat at the dining table. When Bella hung back in the kitchen to help her mother, the only thanks she received was a snapped command for her to go with the others. With her mother in this frame of mind, Bella was hardly going to argue.

It was Lord Charles who cut through the silence as they waited for their food to be served. "It really is wonderful to see you all here — when I heard that the Committee was meeting there was really no way I could miss out on the opportunity to try and *smooth* things over. It really is in everybody's best interests not to repeat the unpleasant scene which I am told took place earlier this week." His words were met with silence from the rest of the Committee, minus its chair; its all-important driving force. Even when Bella's mother did make an appearance, dethroned by Lord Charles, who had taken up the seat at the head of the table, she looked tired and drawn . . . and although Bella hesitated greatly to say it — even to herself — *defeated*.

The starter was strips of smoked salmon with poached eggs. There was a certain reluctance to start into eating given that Bella's mother hadn't yet said so much as a word to them after she had set their plates down. In the end, it was Lord Charles who spoke up, dipping down beneath the table briefly before producing the bottle of champagne he had brought along with him. He broke into a wildly inappropriate grin as he wrestled with the cork. "To a *marvellous* meal — with *marvellous* company!"

The cork sprang forth from the bottle, pinging off the ceiling before coming to rest in some unknown destination. Bella couldn't help but think to herself how one day — maybe weeks from now — her mother would discover that cork lying here or there and how it would be the catalyst for bringing back the memory of today's meal.

It was so unfair how some ghosts of the past seemed impossible to lay to rest, no matter how much time passed, no matter how much distance was run.

Bella's mother appeared to make it her sole mission not to allow anyone time enough away from concentrating on their plates to so much as voice a single syllable. At the sign of the first person nearing the end of their course, she would slip out of the dining room and immediately begin bringing in the plates bearing the next course — on several occasions, especially with Cassandra who was a slow eater, hurrying her guests along and not allowing them the chance to eat everything on their plate.

During these switch-overs, Bella glanced up a few times, doing her best to catch her mother's eye, but — on the choice occasions she did — her mother was straight-lipped, expressionless, apparently unwilling to give anything at all away to her daughter.

When dessert arrived at the table, and was promptly eaten, Bella couldn't help but feel somewhat glad that this car crash of a Sunday dinner was nearing its end.

Once more, she looked to her mother, seeing that she was once again busying herself collecting together plates to take into the kitchen. Bella was determined that this time she wouldn't simply sit by and do nothing at all. She would *act*.

Absorbing the silent table before her, she subtly slipped away.

As she made her way to the kitchen, she heard Lord Charles raise his voice to say something or other.

Throughout the meal, he had tried to make conversation about this, that, or the other, clearly hoping to bring the topic around to his planned golf course outside Normonswold.

But nobody was taking the bait.

Everybody was reluctant to dip their toes in the chilly shallows of Small Talk.

Once again, Bella's mother did her best to block the world out by means of intense activity. She busied herself rinsing the plates then loading them into the dishwasher. Bella knew from experience that this entire cleaning operation would take several hours so she would need to say something soon.

Without another word to her mother, Bella switched the kettle on to boil and then returned briefly to the freezing-cold atmosphere of the dining room to take orders for tea and coffee. Back in the kitchen, as Bella pried through the various cupboards getting the tea bags and pot of coffee she required, she couldn't help but return to Old Couple's Café when she had worked there as a youth. She thought of how no matter what she was going through that day in her personal life she would turn up for work at the café and those smells would take her away . . . *somewhere* else.

"Mum?" Bella said, knowing it was now or never.

Her mother didn't so much as bat an eyelid as she continued to stack the dishwasher.

"Would you like me to ask him to leave?"

Bella's mother concentrated a disproportionately long moment on getting the placement of a plate *just right* before she looked to Bella again. "I think the time for that is long past."

"I'll do it."

Bella's mother's gaze rested on hers. And Bella couldn't help but feel that throbbing, invisible, mother-daughter bond tying them together. "No," her mother finally said. "That wouldn't be the Right Thing to Do."

"Well, the Right Thing to Do, isn't allowing him to swan in wherever he wants, without an invitation. What sort of a message does *that* send?"

Bella's mother said nothing. She remained impossibly still. When she broke out of whatever paralysis gripped her, she glanced down at the half-stacked dishwasher, as if wondering by which hand those plates had got there. Then she looked back at Bella. "I need to front up, don't I? I need to tell him direct? He won't listen to anybody else, will he? Nobody else will even *try*?" Apparently decided now, her mother straightened her back, arched her shoulders, then jutted her chin back. As she stormed from the kitchen, Bella couldn't help but wonder if she hadn't created a monster. And although Bella was of half a mind to shuttle forth from the kitchen, in her mother's wake, she knew — in reality — that the moment had passed. She could already hear her mother's voice bellowing at Lord Charles, demanding that he get out of her house . . . not just her house but the entire *village*.

When Bella finally did take her life into her hands and stuck her head out of the doorway, she was just in time to see Lord Charles's alarmed expression as — necked craned so as not to take his eyes off Indigo Miles — he ushered his personal assistant George in the direction of the front door. If Lord Charles saw Bella at all then he made no sign of recognition.

Before Bella really knew what had happened, Lord Charles and George had departed *Ebbendevor*. In the near distance, she heard the car chunter to life and then crunch its way off over the driveway, leaving them behind.

When Bella's mother emerged from the dining room, Bella saw

that there was a fury in her eyes which Bella had never previously experienced. Neither of them said anything for several long seconds. And then — as if it was the most natural thing in the world — Bella's mother cracked a smile and let loose a cackle any self-respecting witch would've been proud of.

AFTERMATH

*A*lthough Bella knew it was her task to pick up the pieces once her mother had chased Lord Charles and his assistant George from *Ebbendevor*, she couldn't help but feel that she was rendered somewhat redundant. Her mother was going about her tidying-up duties with a sense of undefeatable energy. She swept through the place, whisking up soiled plates and glasses, carrying them into the kitchen. Those who remained watched on, with Robert — chief among them — looking acutely uncomfortable.

Bella was certain that Robert felt torn, knowing instinctively that he should be following his client out of the house, showing some sort of loyalty for the person who was paying him. And yet he had stayed behind, and thus aligned himself with them . . . whatever that really meant. All the same, Bella felt an overwhelming heat warm her entire body.

In the end, after Bella had attempted to establish that her mother was okay for the umpteenth time — and having been flapped away once again — she decided that it was safe for her to leave her in the care of Adiema, Harriet, Cassandra and Dorothy.

Rendered somewhat wrong-footed by her sudden sense of freedom, Bella wasn't sure what to do with herself to begin with. She had half thought of stealing away with Robert to the cabin, but she decided against this plan, seeing the steel-grey skies stretching beyond the grounds of *Ebbendevor* and the raindrops which'd begun to streak the windows.

"You haven't shown me the house yet," Robert said.

Bella wasn't quite sure whether she really wanted to show Robert the house. It took her a few moments to get over herself, to remind herself that he wasn't going to judge her — or whatever it was she was afraid of — as she showed him where she had grown up.

It appeared that they would be going it alone because Woss had curled up into a tight ball and gone to sleep on a comfortable-looking cushion in the corner of the sitting room.

Bella led the way up the staircase, beginning to give a running commentary of all the framed photographic portraits hanging from the walls, but then deciding to give it up and just allow Robert to judge each of the prints on its own merits . . . whatever those merits *were*.

Robert considered each and every one of Bella's school portraits with a slight pout, as if he was trying to mentally peel the years off Bella and reconcile the modern version with the younger one.

When they reached the top of the staircase, Bella felt that the silence had grown somewhat uneasy, and that it was just as she had worried all along — that she and Robert really had nothing else in common aside from mutual physical attraction; and that even this early in their relationship, conversation had run dry.

As they moved from room to room, as Bella did nothing more than gesture at the doorways so that Robert glanced into what had been her bedroom, and then into what was her mother's bedroom, the two guest bedrooms. He said nothing about any of these, but he was clearly not bored. His eyes were active, picking through the details, settling on the odd one, here and there, working it through in his mind. Having shown Robert all the bedrooms, on this floor, Bella began to make her way for the staircase again, to lead him back down to where — no doubt — her mother would be whipping up some hot chocolate, or other refreshing post-Sunday-lunch beverage.

And that was when inspiration struck.

The attic.

She should show him the attic.

And even as the thought appeared in her mind and rested there — so obvious, so logical — she couldn't find the strength to do anything with it right away. And then there seemed to be nothing else for it.

She couldn't speak — somehow it wasn't a case of not being able to find the words, that familiar sensation of just not being able to make conversation about anything — it was a more physical affliction. As if invisible fingers pinched her lips together.

She reached up for the trapdoor, so subtle in the ceiling. She yanked nimbly at the rope which dangled down and the ladder slid towards her, its feet landing gently on the carpet. She looked to Robert, who was now peering upwards, clearly wanting to see where this intriguing ladder led. Already, Bella felt near over-whelmed by the heady scent of the attic — that unshakeable woody odour which sent her tumbling back through the years of her life . . . back to when she had been a child. When she had come here to escape her parents' rows, and then later when she had come up here to escape her mother's tears, or her own heartbreak. And now it felt as if things had come full-circle. She had arrived here with the person who might so easily turn out to be the most important person in her life.

"After you," Bella said, and Robert clambered his way up into the attic.

When they both stood in the cosy space — with the dying daylight sneaking in through the small window which Bella had so often peered out of — there was something wrong. To begin with, it was impossible for Bella to quite put her finger on it. And then it struck her. She glanced back over her shoulder, seeing that they'd left the trapdoor open behind them. She could still make out the tender warm glow of the light below. She shuffled over to the opening and shut the trapdoor. Now it felt better. Now it felt right.

Now she was properly able to absorb her surroundings.

This had almost exclusively been Bella's place. The only sign of anyone else's presence were the few boxes which were stacked up in one of the corners — Christmas decorations, old clothes, and where Bella had temporarily kept her possessions while she had briefly been living back here with her mother. The only piece of furniture in the attic was a beaten and battered armchair, missing its legs, with stuffing bursting from its seams, and a small coffee table which was scratched and scraped. Although it seemed humble — *far* humbler than the rest of the house, at least — this space had meant the world to Bella when she had been younger. And even now, she felt the tingling sensation pass through her veins as she stood here. This had been a safe place for her; her own personal *refuge* . . . and now she had brought someone into this place . . . now she had let someone *in*.

When Robert reached out and placed his open palms against the sides of her neck, she didn't tremble out of fear. It was longing. The feeling of having held a desire for so long that she had begun to believe that it would never truly come to pass . . . that faint, almost invisible line which divided dream from reality. The space that Humble Greetings occupied.

Before Bella knew it herself, one of the many fantasies she had envisaged while up here in the attic began to play out.

Robert eased her dress strap down her shoulder. She felt as if she was leaving her skin behind. As if he was unwrapping that which protected her very soul. His breath was warm and moist, and it smelled wonderful. His hold on her was firm, unfaltering. There was nothing unsteady about Robert. Nothing *raw* about him. He was pure aggression, channelled into a straight edge. As Bella stood before Robert, naked, she followed his eyes as they stalked all over her body, taking her in in this quiet, out-of-the-way space.

There were distant voices, off in the house.

Happy voices.

This was the sensation which Bella had so often craved. That things might be normal — that the atmosphere clinging to the house might be something other than a drab *grey*.

Well, the house certainly didn't seem *grey* right now.

Not with Robert here. He was the Great Illuminator. He was warming her from the outside in — his hands swift and efficient, finding the fastest way to her heart.

As Bella moved them down to the armchair, she ran her hands over Robert's abdomen, and his arms, feeling his powerful, relaxed muscles. He wasn't just the man she needed right now. He was the man who she had been looking for her entire life. It was so strange that she had had to come back home to discover that . . . that the person she had sought out for so long was where she had started her life. And that she had brought him back to where it had all begun. At least for her.

As he took hold of her with his gentle strength, she sank her teeth into her bottom lip, feeling her pulse. Her heart beat up in her throat. It made it impossible to think . . . and she welcomed the sensation. She welcomed this . . . this new life.

Eyes half open, Bella fixed her stare out the attic window, seeing the sun disappearing below the line of trees, setting the fledgling flower buds and newly emerged leaves alive with golden rays. Her whole mind had locked down now. She was escaping from Normonswold . . . escaping the *Earth* . . . seeking out that imaginary place which she had begun to believe didn't exist at all.

She was so glad she had never stopped looking.

24

CAUGHT IN THE LURCH

*T*here weren't many days when Robert could honestly recall waking up with a smile pressed across his lips. But today had certainly been one of them. He hadn't had one of those nightmares of his in the longest time — no more of those impossibly gloomy corridors stretching off into forever. It seemed almost as if he was incapable of negative thoughts. Almost as if he was . . . *happy.*

It was just like a film how everything played out — birds chittering in the trees, sun beaming down, everything seemed somehow more vibrant. He smiled at the world and it smiled right back at him. When Robert finally did manage to get himself out of the bed he was staying in at the Thicket Arms, he was planning a leisurely morning — partaking of the generous Full English Breakfast offered then taking a short walk with Woss about the village before going out to the construction site to see how things were getting on. However these plans were rendered ridiculous almost right away by the thunking knocks at his door.

Robert pressed his fingers into his temples, perhaps subconsciously trying to get the smile off his face so that he wouldn't look like a complete moron to whoever was standing on the other side.

From where he slept in the corner, Woss opened a weary eye before deciding that it wasn't worth waking up for whoever the guest might be and drifted back off to sleep.

As happy with his current state as Robert imagined he was going to get, he shifted out from beneath his duvet, crossed the room, and opened the door. He was met with Lord Charles's intense stare. The two of them looked at one another for the longest time before Lord Charles spoke. Although Robert had expected Lord Charles to be in a furious mood, for him to be dealing with how he had been thrown out of yesterday's dinner party while Robert had stayed unfaithfully, he was taken off guard at just how measured Lord Charles's tone of voice was; how despite whatever anger he might've been feeling, he kept his outward appearance fully under control.

"Good morning, Robert."

"Good morning, Lord Charles."

Lord Charles prodded out his tongue, resting it on his bottom lip. This was a gesture which Lord Charles often practised whenever he was in deep thought about some issue or another. It never lasted for very long — because Lord Charles didn't remain indecisive about any one issue for a second longer than he had to. His eyes picked out Robert's. His gaze penetrated him in a way many people in the city would imitate, but Robert could tell that there was nothing imitative in Lord Charles's gaze

. . .

"I just wanted to reaffirm your commitment to the project, Robert."

Robert stood stock still. He supposed that he had expected an inquisition along these lines, albeit a touch more subtle. All the same, he had his response. "We've signed a contract, haven't we?"

At this statement, any trace of a smile which might have lined Lord Charles's lips evaporated completely. When he spoke again, Robert expected Lord Charles to break out into a fury, but his tone remained as cool as ever.

"Yes, Robert, yes we did. And if there's anything that I'd heard repeated ad nauseam by those who recommended you, it was that you are as professional as anyone.

Committed to getting the job done."

Robert felt that — despite the positive connotation of what Lord Charles was saying — there was a somewhat sharp twist to his tone. Almost a *mocking* tone. As if there was something off about being 'committed' . . . or perhaps it was the utilitarian nature of his relationship with the project.

With any project.

Having worked with more obscenely rich people than he cared to count, Robert had come to see that — more often than not — the project became far more than a business proposal. It almost always ended up being some sort of a personal totem. As self-indulgent as having one's appearance carved out of marble . . . sometimes Robert wondered why they didn't just do something like that rather than dress up their arrogance in the form of a business plan.

Lord Charles cocked his head to one side, as if by simply seeing Robert from a different angle he might be able to garner something new about him — his true nature. "Is there anything you'd like to tell me, Robert? Anything which you'd like to *ask* me?"

Robert's first reaction was to tell Lord Charles that there was *nothing* at all . . . he was serious about getting the job done and being finished with this relationship, with this golf resort . . . but the more he attempted to keep his lips pressed tightly together, the more he found it a struggle. One which was impossible to rise above.

"What's so important about Normonswold?" Robert asked.

"What?"

"Why is your heart so set on building the golf resort here — just outside this village?"

Lord Charles didn't look angry, or at all affected by what Robert had asked. But he did seem to be using a great deal of his mental strength to form a response. "Does it really matter?"

"Yes."

Lord Charles glanced directly at Robert, then switched his attention to the window, looking out into the street, down at the country lane which twisted through the centre of Normonswold. "When I was a child, my parents would bring me here . . . to Normonswold . . . they were . . . they were . . ." at this point, Robert was ready for anything; for Lord Charles to break down into tears, or for Lord Charles to turn on his heel and leave in a blaze of fury "they were . . . such happy times."

Lord Charles slowly turned his gaze back onto Robert, as if Robert was going to challenge him about this claim. As if he was going to argue that Lord Charles was merely manipulating him. That he was twisting him and goading him, trying to bring him into line.

Attempting to get him back on His Side.

But when Robert looked on Lord Charles, he couldn't help but see a profound sadness there. Something deep and impossible to remove. There was no response to him other than pity. And a sense of perhaps wanting to help him out . . . to help him feel *better*.

Robert supposed the whole adage of money being unable to

buy happiness was truer than was usually given credit. Although Lord Charles was attempting to prove it false with all his strength.

"Do you think the resort will make you happy?"

"I think that it will make me *happier* than I am right now."

There was a thoroughly hollow tone to Lord Charles's voice now, as if he was on the point of breaking down. Robert was unsure whether he would be able to handle that. He supposed that situation would be one which would require the specialist skills of Lord Charles's personal assistant, George.

"You're seeing that girl, aren't you, Robert?"

Robert came back to the present with a thud. "Uh, yes," he replied, unable to think of anything else to say.

Lord Charles merely nodded at this statement. "A clever girl — her potential might be wasted in such a backwater place as Normonswold."

Robert wanted to explain to Lord Charles how Bella had already been to the Big City, and how it hadn't helped her to fulfil whatever 'potential' might be 'wasted' . . . then again people like Lord Charles — no matter how hard they attempted to be seen to appeal to the nobler motives — never seemed completely able to empathise with those who had different goals, different dreams, different measures of success.

Out in the hall, there was the sound of footsteps, Lord Charles and Robert glanced back. George — Lord Charles's personal assistant — crept into view, and then, with a knowing look over the two of them, immediately grasping that they were not to be disturbed, he continued on his way down the stairs; to go and wait for his master as faithfully as Woss waited for Robert.

Lord Charles turned to Robert. It felt as if any of the sincere feeling between the two of them which had existed until a matter of moments ago was lost . . . not that Robert was at all concerned.

In fact, he much preferred that things remained on business terms not just with Lord Charles but with any of his clients. It helped to avoid complications further down the line. Unpleasant situations.

"I just wanted your assurance — your *word* — that you are still committed to the project. That your head hasn't been turned."

Robert held himself still. He thought about the question before answering. And it was harder to answer than it ever had been. But, all the same, he *knew* the answer. "I'm still committed," he said. "One hundred percent."

"Good," Lord Charles replied, with the flicker of a smile, and then, his grin becoming broader, he reached out and clapped his hand onto Robert's shoulder, signalling the end of their Serious Chat, and a return to more affable interactions. "I'm so glad to hear it, Robert. I have to admit, for a moment, for a few seconds this morning, I managed to convince myself otherwise. But I know that you are the consummate professional. I know that you can be trusted. And with something which is so dear to me."

Once Lord Charles had disappeared down the hallway, headed off to go and meet George, Robert wasn't entirely sure exactly what he had committed to. He looked to Woss, whose eyes were half open beneath their lids. The only witness to this conversation. When Woss had satisfied himself that Robert wasn't going to take him on 'walkies' in the immediate future, he closed his eyes and drifted back off to his doggy daydreams.

Some days Robert wondered if he wouldn't be better off as a dog.

25

SUCCESS BREEDS SUCCESS

*S*unshine streamed in through the windows of the studio as Bella worked on fresh copy to accompany Cassandra's latest illustrations. It was only when she felt a lingering ache in her cheeks that she reached up and touched her face, realising that she was smiling broadly, uncontrollably. When she got up to make some coffee around mid-afternoon, she realised that she hadn't been this happy — this *content* — with her life for the longest time. It wasn't since she had first left Normonswold behind that she had felt like this. It was a new sense of freedom. This was the first time that she had *known* that it had been a good idea to leave the Big City behind and to return home.

No, it hadn't simply been a 'good' idea . . . it had been a *great* idea.

It was impossible to think that she had had any misapprehensions going into Humble . . . any misapprehensions about taking over what had once been Florianette Rutherford's home. It was just as her mother had put it to her — a way of continuing Florianette's legacy . . . a way for her to keep a creative well at the centre of Normonswold.

Then there was the question of Robert Rutherford. Where did she start with that? She decided that — if she wanted to get any work done that day — it was better that she didn't start with it at all.

And, creation, and love, apart, Bella had checked her email that morning to discover that there were hundreds of messages. To begin with, she had dreaded the sight, wondering if one of her old contacts had managed to track her down, and that she was being subjected to some kind of an online intervention — an attempt to drag her back to London, back to the life which she had become tired with, and the job she had come to loathe.

But it wasn't anything of the kind.

The emails, as it turned out, were from shop owners — *distributors* — who were interested in stocking Humble cards. And it was then that a different sort of fear overtook her. A fear that this was, well . . . *too much* . . . she thought about the printer which they had in one of the small rooms of the house, and how it had seemed almost monstrously big when it had first arrived; but how it now seemed impossibly small given the scope of the task. And Bella began to wonder if she wasn't going to be forced to turn some of these people down.

Previously she would have panicked. She might've pretended that the emails didn't exist at all, or otherwise fool herself into believing that she couldn't cope — that she had made a great error in this venture of hers. But she had places to turn now.

After a brief discussion with Cassandra, in which Cassandra had a similar reaction to the quantity of email orders they needed to deal with, Bella had no hesitation in picking up the phone and getting in touch with Robert. As she held the phone to her ear, she felt her heart throbbing in her throat and a slight sheen of perspiration cling to her forehead. There was something about Robert — whenever she thought about him — that sent her whirling back to her days as a schoolgirl; all skittish and callow.

When Robert agreed that he would drop round, Bella felt more apprehensive than when she had been staring at the bottomless pile of emails alone. She had to use logical arguments to convince herself that this was right — that, soon, everything would be sorted out once Robert had dispensed his help and advice.

As she gravitated towards the kitchen, Bella finally understood one of her mother's nervous foibles. How her mother would hover about in the kitchen, picking up a mug here, or a teapot there, clearly attempting to divine the state of her guest's mind — wanting to be able to make them at home straight away and, in so doing, put herself at ease too. That was wishful thinking, though, because to say that Bella was hot under the collar at the prospect of Robert's visit was to put it lightly . . .

By the time there was a knock at the door, Bella hadn't actually got around to doing anything about the whole beverage situation. She had never been able to finally settle on either tea or coffee, and there was no point to starting on sweet treats at this late stage.

She took a moment to compose herself, looked to Cassandra — who suddenly made herself scarce, slipping out through the back door, and into the garden — and then went to let Robert in. As he stood framed in the doorway, Bella could hardly believe her eyes.

In his overcoat, with his hair brushing his shoulders, it was as if he dominated the landscape outside — as if he was a giant who she was inviting in from the cold. When she took a step back into the house, she had to remind herself not to trip up. Their eyes locked together. And, sooner than she could react, he reached down for her hands at her sides, entangling his fingers with hers, and staring into her eyes.

"I love you, Bella."

Bella's heart fluttered up to her throat again. It prevented her from being able to speak at all. And then she swallowed hard. She twisted her neck upwards, and pressed her lips firmly against his, losing herself in the moment.

When Bella surfaced, cheeks flushed from the overwhelmingly hot glow which encompassed the two of them, it felt as if her mind itself was doing backflips. They were lying wrapped in blankets on the floor of the studio, where Bella and Cassandra had spent so much time getting their greetings cards *just right*.

She pressed herself up against Robert's chest, feeling his tight muscles relaxed. And his heart beating slow and steady. She told him about the problems she was having with capacity. How there seemed to be more orders for her to deal with than she could ever manage in a lifetime. Robert said nothing to this, only holding her.

When Bella had been murmuring quietly for what felt like fifteen, twenty minutes, she glanced up to take in his face, wondering if he might not have drifted off to sleep. However, she saw that although his eyelids drooped heavy, he was very much awake. Only when she reached a natural pause, the stage of what she was outlining in which she could no longer see any way forward, did he speak up.

"You'll need to outsource," he said, as if it was that simple. "You'll need to find somewhere else to do the printing — perhaps somewhere in the city, closer to where the distributors are."

Although this seemed obvious to Bella in retrospect, she had to admit that she hadn't made the leap. She had been so overwhelmed by the sheer quantity of orders facing her that she hadn't been able to get past the block. And then another issue struck.

"Will it, you know, still hold true to Humble's mission statement if we decide to outsource printing?"

Robert drew in a heavy breath. "That's for you to decide, I suppose."

Bella felt her whole body contract. There was something about today — something about Robert's tone — which seemed off. But then hadn't he said that he *loved* her when he had arrived on the doorstep? Was that what had her all aflutter? Unable to keep her silly thoughts from dancing off in twisting spirals, it was then that it felt as if the spell was broken, at least for the time being.

Bella got up and dressed, while Robert did the same. She took special care to fold up the blanket before laying it down on a bench where it had rested before the two of them had come into the studio. When they returned to the kitchen, Bella couldn't help but notice that Robert seemed a touch impatient. He kept on glancing at his watch. It sent a gentle, warm wave through her when he looked her in the eye as he smiled.

"I've got a meeting with Lord Charles at four," he said. "I'm a little on edge about it." He shook his head slightly and the smile slipped from his lips. "Actually, I'm a bit more than on *edge* — I'm greatly uneasy."

Bella thought of asking Robert to elaborate, but, in the end, she decided against doing so. She had to understand that — at least for the time being — Robert had two lives, one with her, and one with Lord Charles, who was his client. It would be folly to mix the two of them. That would be a recipe for disaster. Even though neither of them had said anything in words, they both acknowledged that they would just need to put up with the conflict until one thing —

the lovers' fling or the business relationship — came to an end . . .
and then Bella wondered just what she meant by 'fling'; was that all
this was?

It made her heart ache.

And her whole being want to know where she stood.

But she decided against voicing any of these concerns with
Robert. He, after all, had enough on his mind to contend with.

Before leaving, Robert asked if he could look over Humble's
accounts. When the two of them had managed to prise themselves
apart for brief moments, weeks earlier, Robert had set about the
task of formalising all of the hopes and dreams which Bella had so
lovingly — but also so illogically — busied herself with. He had
given structure to everything in the business; starting with the
relationship between Bella and Cassandra, and ending somewhere
around accounting for every single drawing pencil they had on the
premises for business purposes. He had been coming in — once a
week — to look through all of the receipts and invoices that'd been
generated, checking Bella's work, making sure that she hadn't
made any errors with her sums. Realising that he was running late,
he stuffed the receipts and accounts into his briefcase alongside his
laptop, kissed Bella goodbye at the door, told her that he would
look over them that night. Then he ventured out into the length-
ening evening.

For the longest time, Bella felt a strange sense of loss.

As if she had seen Robert for the last time.

It was an almost overwhelming feeling of foreboding.

2 6

A TREACHEROUS DEAL

*I*t wasn't too often that Robert felt flustered, but he certainly felt that way today. He liked everything in his life to follow a sense of logic and order — he abhorred the feeling of things slipping out of his control. And he always strived to be better than he had been the previous day. Now, though, he would have openly admitted to anybody who cared to ask that he had lost control . . . that he was *freewheeling*.

As he brought his car boot down, he almost hit Woss on the head, who had risen on his hind paws to look out at him from the back seat. Robert apologise to Woss through the glass, and Woss gave him one of those looks reserved for whenever he had been given a Good Telling Off. He promised himself that he would make things up to Woss later on — that he would take him off for a good long walk later. There was more light in the evenings now, although the weather still carried a brutal chill.

Robert's briefcase knocked against his thigh as he upped his pace, making for the canvas tent on the outside of the construction

171

site. He saw that — as usual — the Normonswold Village Committee had staked out a place about twenty yards from the entrance of the site, along the road. After some fraught negotiation, Robert had managed to come to a compromise with them, that instead of the Village Committee preventing traffic from accessing the site, they could stop any vehicle passing along the road and hand them a leaflet about preserving the village. This seemed much more preferable to Lord Charles's idea, which had been to get in touch with the local constabulary — to get the police to break up the protests. It amazed Robert just how swiftly people's minds could be changed, or if not changed then their thoughts greatly altered, if you just paid attention to their concerns.

If you just *listened* to them.

And that was really all he had done.

Nothing special.

Just listen.

And now construction was back on track.

Lord Charles was already waiting for Robert, looking extremely irritable, checking his watch, apparently having been pacing up and down beside the tent window with a view onto the entire building site. "You're late," Lord Charles said.

"I'm sorry, I don't know where the time . . ."

Lord Charles swept his arm over the camp table, two chairs drawn up to it. "Sit."

Robert did as he was told, resting his briefcase on his lap.

Out of the window, Lord Charles had narrowed his focus upon a pair of large, dirty-grey tanks which were being lowered into the ground by the contractors.

Not knowing what else to say — and vaguely thinking that it

might ease the tension in the room to make conversation, Robert said, "Septic tanks?"

Lord Charles smiled grimly. "Sanitation, a necessary evil." Then Lord Charles eyed him for the longest time before any trace of a smile vanished from his lips. "Tell it to me straight, Robert, are we on track with the resort or are things as bad as I think they are?"

Normally Robert would have no hesitation in delivering bad news, but today was different. He felt rushed. He felt a little panicked. As if things were drifting out of control. As if he had got himself into something he had never imagined . . . it was the dawning realisation that he had somehow sleep walked into something which he had attempted to resist for his entire life: mixing his professional life with his personal one.

"Actually, Lord Charles," Robert began, his voice a touch shaky. "I was going to float the possibility of my withdrawal from the project. It's with . . ."

Lord Charles held up a hand. Then he closed his eyes tightly, squeezing the bridge of his nose as if he was suffering from a sudden, severe migraine. Lord Charles assumed this pose for the best part of a minute before he looked at Robert again — Robert was unsure whether or not he should still be there. He had known far less volatile figures than Lord Charles who would take exception to their 'underlings' not interpreting subtle clues for them to get out.

Lord Charles, though, did not appear to be angry.

In fact, he was smiling . . .

"It would be very convenient, wouldn't it, Robert?"

Robert still said nothing. He was waiting for the eruption. It would be any second now. There was no way that Lord Charles would be able to keep a lid on his emotion. Not for much longer.

Not when he was *this close* to achieving what he had set out to gain . . . not when someone threatened to stand in his way.

"And what if I rejected your withdrawal? What would you do then?"

Robert breathed in deeply. His thoughts were so scattered that it was difficult to get his brain to commune with his mouth. But he did the best he could. "I feel that I have compromised the project. That I hold a personal stake in it — and that it would not be professional of me to continue my association . . ." Robert didn't fully close his mouth, wondering if he shouldn't add something more, but in the end he couldn't form any sound in his throat.

Lord Charles arched his shoulders and glanced down at the tips of his shoes. "I don't see any problem. If there was one then I would have mentioned it, don't you think?"

"Yes," Robert replied, beginning to feel somewhat exasperated now, "but it's not just a question of what you think — it is what I morally and ethically believe. I want to do a good job, a professional job, and at the moment I think that's compromised."

" 'At the moment' ?"

Unable to maintain his poker face, Robert winced. Normally, he was all too aware of the words which came out of his mouth, but today they had got the better of him. All the more evidence — if more evidence was what he needed — that his thinking was correct. That he wasn't fully focused on achieving his client's aims.

"Are those the accounts?" Lord Charles asked, glancing at the briefcase lying across Robert's lap.

Robert nodded.

Lord Charles breathed in deeply, and then snapped his fingers at the briefcase.

Robert handed it over.

Lord Charles laid the briefcase down on the table between

them, opening it so that the lid concealed the contents from Robert — as if Robert didn't well know just what was inside. Lord Charles's gaze flitted over a few items within before he glanced up. "This is your personal laptop, is it not?"

"It is. Everything you need is on there. You're welcome to transfer your files off."

Lord Charles looked up, turning his attention over the top of Robert's head. It was only when Robert turned in his seat that he realised Lord Charles's personal assistant — George — was standing in the doorway. There was no need for words. Lord Charles snapped the briefcase shut and George took the briefcase from his employer.

Once George had left the tent, Lord Charles smiled at Robert. "It shouldn't take more than a couple of days, then you'll have it back, in the meantime you should go home — I don't want to see you around here. You look tired, Robert. You need to relax. Come back when you're good and ready. When you've had a *proper* chance to think things through. Then we'll talk about whether or not we should continue our working relationship."

Feeling struck by a kind of daze, Robert shifted to his feet, then made his way out of the tent. As he plodded along the grassy verge of the muddy track, he felt an enormous weight lifting off his shoulders. It was almost like the feeling he recalled when — in the first day of spring — his mother would throw open all the windows and allow the fresh air in.

He had done the right thing.

Said the right things.

And now he was on the road to being free of Lord Charles and his plans . . . once he had got through the cooling-off period.

A NEW DAWN

*B*ella woke with the sunrise. As she went down to the kitchen to put the coffee on — whoever of Cassandra or Bella was up and about was in charge of putting on the first pot of coffee — she felt a clean warmth clinging to the air. All the signs suggested that this was going to be the first proper day of spring . . . that it would be the first day of warm, pure sunshine for what felt like months and months. And she couldn't wait.

With the coffee brewed, leaving behind enough for Cassandra and a few refills throughout the morning, she made it down to the studio where she went about dashing off her first few lines of copy of the day. She always liked to work first thing, when her mind was still fresh. She felt as if her thoughts came forth from some kind of a bottomless well at this time — everything was smooth and easy — whereas later it would be nothing but stodgy and awkward. This worked well with the routine the two of them had established, too. Because Cassandra preferred to work during the night, it meant that each morning when Bella woke up there would be a fresh stack of sketches, all ready for Bella to scribble out her accompanying copy.

The hours passed quickly, and it wasn't until a little after nine o'clock that she surfaced to go and get some more coffee. As she was pouring out a fresh cup, she heard the giveaway *rustle* of the post falling through the letterbox. She went to fetch it. She separated the personal post from the business correspondence, then set about opening it.

All of the post was standard fare until she reached the very last letter.

As Bella slit open the envelope and retrieved the folded-up piece of paper from within, she didn't feel that anything was different. It was only when she read the first few lines of the first paragraph that she nearly spilled her coffee down her front. She read them over and over again:

. . . we wish to place an order of 500,000 units.

It was hard to get past that part of the letter. She kept scanning it back over again, as if trying to tease out some alternative meaning. As if there had to be some other explanation for that line. She looked over the letter, trying to get a sense of the timeframe involved — but, again, there was nothing which stood out. It seemed that this supplier wanted their order as soon as it was ready to ship . . . if it was *ever* ready to ship . . . *five hundred thousand* cards!

Bella forced herself to calm down, sorting the rest of the business correspondence into piles, somehow trying to squeeze a modicum of normality from the morning. When she got through with wasting as much time as she could manage, she returned to the letter which had put her into such a bizarre frame of mind first thing in the morning. It was then that she felt Robert's common sense kicking in — when she recalled one of his many lessons. 'In business,' he had said, 'anything which seems out of the ordinary probably is.'

Bella glanced at the letterhead, took note of the number, and picked up the phone.

Bella was shaking by the time she got off the phone.

She had called the business up, speaking to the person in charge of placing the order. They had confirmed to her, without fanfare, that they did indeed intend to place the order as it had been set out in the letter. They would send through another email confirmation that day to ensure they had the required documentation — so that Bella and Cassandra would know what they needed to supply. They also confirmed that they wanted the shipment as soon as possible.

As soon as possible!

Bella remained still for another few minutes, feeling the caffeine drip about her veins, making her irritable and alert in equal measure. And then she thrust herself to her feet.

She woke Cassandra with a practised few shakes. There had been more than a half a dozen exciting occasions which'd led Bella to doing so, and Cassandra had always been glad that Bella had woken her up — at least when the effects of the Morning Grumps had worn off. Cassandra sat up in bed, her eyelids dropping and her mouth seemingly stuck in a never-ending yawn. Bella told her the news in six seconds flat. Then the two of them sat in silence for what felt like an eternity. Both trying to grasp just what it meant for the immediate future.

There was only one clear answer:

Get up and get working!

Again, there was no need for words, Bella and Cassandra knew their roles. They headed down to the studio, sifting through the latest batch, trying to work out which of the new designs they were going to send to the printer that afternoon. Which ones would work the best with such a large bulk order. It wasn't long before Bella realised that this was the big break which Humble had been waiting for — it wasn't worthwhile holding anything back. They had to put *everything* out there . . . show the world what Humble Greetings was and what it represented. There was no time for half measures.

And so, at around midday, after Bella and Cassandra had hurriedly finalised a few designs which they had been close to finishing, and slipped out older designs from their files to be reprinted, Bella called up the printer they had decided to work with and then sent over the templates for them to go about processing.

That done, Bella felt as if she had run two marathons back to back.

She fell onto the sofa, her whole body limp.

Cassandra fell onto the cushions beside her.

"Do we need to do anything else?" Cassandra finally asked.

"I . . . don't think so . . . it's weird, isn't it? When we were printing stuff out here, at least we could see the progress — at least we had the peace of mind that things were getting *done*. Now, though . . . it's just weird."

When Bella tried to get to her feet, Cassandra reached out and wrapped her fingers about her forearm, preventing her going any further. All Cassandra had to do was shake her head. Even without words, Bella understood perfectly what Cassandra was getting at . . . . they were *not* going to ask the printer if they could watch ten thousand cards being printed.

Bella didn't protest.

She was much too tired.

"What now, then?" Bella asked.

"Let's celebrate."

It didn't take long for Bella's mother — along with Adiema, Harriet and Dorothy — to show up on the doorstep. And from there it was a significantly shorter wait for the first champagne cork to pop. Even as she was surrounded by smiling, happy faces, Bella couldn't help but feel that the situation would be greatly improved by Robert being there. When she had called him, though, she hadn't been able to get through. She might try again in a few minutes, when she —

"Bella! Bella!"

Bella turned to see her mother, seeing that she had somehow clambered onto the kitchen table, and that she held the bottle of champagne down at her side, as if she was a knight of the realm, her sword dangling towards the ground. Bella had the vague notion of suggesting to her mother that the table might not be entirely stable for her to stand on, but she decided against this. She wasn't in favour of reversing the mother-daughter dynamic any earlier than was strictly necessary. Not seeing that she could get away with doing anything else, she allowed her mother to refill the flute until champagne spilled out over the rim.

"A toast!" her mother called out above them.

Bella was glad to see that there were others who openly wore concerned gazes across their faces; worried that Bella's mother might topple off the table. Already Bella was thinking about the trip to the hospital, and then the conversation with the doctors to explain *just how* this had happened.

It seemed, though, that the normal rules of gravity and every reaction having an equal and opposite reaction just didn't apply to her mother any longer.

"To victory!" her mother cried.

Not knowing what else to do, Bella raised her glass into the air and joined the others in bellowing, "To victory!" in chorus.

They drank long into the night.

28

DOWN TO EARTH

*I*t wasn't until three days later that Bella truly surfaced from the celebrations which'd accompanied Humble's first bulk order. It was a phone call that did it, as always seemed to be the case.

For some reason, she expected it to be Robert — that although he had been missing in action for days now, he might have seen sense and decided to get in touch.

Maybe he was calling to congratulate her.

But when she picked up the phone, it was an unfamiliar voice on the other end.

The line wasn't good, either, so she had difficulty in making out exactly what was being said. "Miss Miles . . . an order . . . Humble Greetings . . ."

Bella felt her chest contract, squeezing her ribs together. She felt a buzz pass through her bloodstream. This was it . . . the moment she had been waiting for . . . so soon now all of those cards would be making their way out into the world. That was what the major distributor had promised. That the order of five hundred thousand units would be sent on to shops around the globe. This would change everything. Although Bella understood nowhere near as much about business as Robert did — and nor would she want to — she understood the concept that increased exposure led to increased demand.

A virtuous or vicious circle, depending on how she looked at it.

"Sorry, can you repeat that?" she said, into the phone. "I can hardly hear you."

More garbled muttering on the other end of the line.

"Sorry?"

When Bella looked up from where she was sat at the kitchen table, she saw that Cassandra was standing in the doorway. Over the past few days, whenever the phone had rung and Bella had gone to answer, Cassandra had got up to keep a close eye on her . . . apparently wanting to find out the news as soon as Bella.

Finally, the line came clear for a smattering of seconds. "Is this Humble Greetings?"

"Yes, it is."

"There is a problem. We have received an order for greetings cards, ten thousand units? We never . . . never . . ." the line became garbled again, but Bella already knew where this conversation was headed ". . . if you could . . . arrange for the . . ."

The line cut out.

Bella sat stunned for several seconds.

And then the phone rang again.

"Hello?"

"Hi, is that Humble Greetings?"

"Yes, Bella speaking."

"We have received an order for fifteen thousand units this morning, but we never placed an order with yourselves. Please would you advise on how we should go about returning these . . . these . . . greetings cards?"

It felt as if someone had punched Bella in the ribcage. She got through the rest of the call, doing her best to keep her tone of voice level, unflinching.

She had hardly finished with that call when the phone rang again.

It was another distributor . . . having received an unwanted order.

A dizzy spell struck Bella. On impulse, she hung up. She dug around the kitchen in a frenzy, searching for the letter from the original distribution company. She uncovered it, dialled up the number.

No response.

Just ringing.

She tried again.

Ringing again.

She waited a fraction longer.

The phone line went dead.

She was aware of her breathing becoming shallow and difficult to control. Of her vision beginning to blur and blacken about the edges. When she started to feel faint, she grabbed herself back from the edge, determined not to go to ground like some over-wrought nineteenth-century courtier.

"Okay," she muttered to herself, laying the phone down on the table in front of her, "okay, okay . . ."

Cassandra was still standing in the doorway, but now she was staring at the floor.

There was no need for words.

The two of them knew what this meant.

What *else* could it mean?

They had been tricked.

And Humble Greetings was doomed.

Bella went back to bed — there didn't seem to be anything else which she could logically do. Cassandra did the same. The two of them sealing themselves off in their own solitary spaces, as if they needed to grieve for what was about to come to pass.

Five hundred thousand units.

Half a million units.

There was no way that they would be able to bounce back from this.

The hit was just too *massive*.

To start with, there was nowhere they could sensibly store so many cards. But that was by the by. The biggest problem was the hit to cash flow. Bella had had to take out several loans in order to fund the order — to get that many cards printed up and to the buyer. But now the buyer had pulled out. And left her and Cassandra high and dry.

Bella felt a lot of things all at the same time. She felt terrible for having led Cassandra on this merry dance, all the way down the garden path . . . to here.

What were they going to do now?

Well, actually, there was a simple answer to that question.

Nothing.

They could *do* nothing at all.

Humble Greetings was finished.

It would just be a case of sorting through the rubble, working out all of the formal arrangements for winding down the company. She was glad that she had Robert now — she could admit that much. Something like this would have seemed impossible to go through without someone close to her who knew what they were talking about. And it was just then — with Robert on her mind — that the thought struck.

Suddenly she was hit by a sense of urgency, that there was something which she had yet to fully acknowledge. An angle which she hadn't yet fully reconnoitred.

She leaped down the staircase, taking a couple of steps at a time, and she made it down into the studio. She flung open one of the cupboards and foraged about within, hoping to find what she was looking for. But there was nothing there. She recalled the day when Robert had brought over a three-tiered tray into which she was supposed to sort her pending filing — all of the invoices and expenses which Robert would look through later.

There was nothing in the trays now.

And then she thought about the last time she had looked in the cupboard . . . actually, it hadn't been her who had looked in the cupboard.

It had been Robert.

Before he had gone to the meeting with Lord Charles.

Now — *now* — everything suddenly made sense.

Everything fell into place.

Unable to control herself any longer, Bella snatched up her phone and dialled Robert's number. She tried again and again but it was impossible to get through. He hadn't stopped by to see her in what felt like forever, and now he was avoiding her calls. Bella braced herself, trying to get her mind back together, and then dialled one final time.

This time she got through.

She heard his breathing on the other end of the line for along few moments. "Bella?" he said, finally.

"How could you do this to me?"

"Do what, Bella?"

Now she felt her throat constrict. She tried not to allow it to affect her voice, but — at the same time — it felt as if there was no holding back the driving emotion . . . the indomitable sadness. She pushed herself through. Told him what had happened, with the spoof order, and how it would finish Humble once and for all.

"Bella, please, listen to me — it's not what you think."

She held the phone to her ear. Although it seemed impossible to believe that it could be anything *but* what it looked like, she was prepared to hear him out.

"I . . . was taking the papers . . . to Lord Charles . . . actually, I was pulling out of the project" — she felt the manic smile in his voice — "I'd made my mind up, I couldn't do it any longer. Doesn't that make sense?" He paused for a long time and when he spoke again, his tone was hurried, as if he had seen the finish line in sight and his instinct was to rush for it in long, unthinking bounds. "I wanted to hand back the accounts to Lord Charles, so that we could finish our business relationship. I forgot that I had Humble's accounts inside there. Lord Charles must have seen them. And he saw a way to hurt you . . . a way of hurting the people who were getting in the way of his plans. And he took it."

Bella allowed Robert the time to elaborate further, but he seemed finished. She held on for another few seconds. Then she could restrain herself no longer. "I don't know what would be worse . . . that you did this intentionally, or that you were so careless with something so important to me."

29

WAKING UP

*I*t was a little after ten in the morning as Bella walked alone through the woods. It was a few days after Robert had declared his love for her . . . and a couple of days closer still to the day that he had betrayed her.

The morning was beautiful, fresh, with raindrops still clinging to the leaves of the trees. Sunrays were just beginning to burst through the foliage, warming her skin. She knew that they were well into spring now, and that summer was just around the corner.

Not having anything else to plough her energy into — she had sent Cassandra home to her parents since it was about as depressing to do work on Humble as it would've been to lovingly maintain a sinking ship — Bella had joined her mother whole-heartedly in opposing Lord Charles's project. He was throttling along at full-speed.

One day, when Lord Charles had arrived at the site for a flying visit, Bella had confronted him directly — asked him why he had ruined her dream, why he had thought it necessary to squash her start-up with his shoe sole. He had just smiled broadly at her and tapped the bridge of his nose.

And that had twisted the anger — like a knife — in Bella's gut.

But it had also made her more determined.

She and her mother were organising events almost every single day in opposition to Lord Charles's resort. Now that Bella didn't have Humble to spend her time on, she had even managed to rope in the committees of several adjacent villages; somehow selling them the premise that whatever could happen to Normonswold could just as easily happen to them. That a victory for Normonswold would be a victory for all. Perhaps all of those skills of negotiation she had picked up from her time in the city weren't wasted after all.

As Bella carried on along the dirt path, winding through the trees, she recalled the time she and Robert had spent together in the woods. It seemed such a long time ago.

Another lifetime.

Like the life she had left behind in the city.

And just as confined to the past.

When she brought the cabin into view, it looked impossibly beautiful — incredibly *idyllic* — in the brightening sunshine. Bird-song filled her ears as she approached. She listened to how her footsteps crunched across the forest floor.

She sensed her body beginning to relax.

She was tense — so, so tense.

It was strange to think that there were people who thought of living out their dreams as being somehow relaxing — a chance to 'be your own boss' — but that couldn't have been any further from the truth. Bella knew now that whatever she did — every success, every failure — was entirely upon her. And failure truly dominated everything now.

Bella was thinking of taking a walk around the lake — it had been over a decade since she had last done so — when she spotted motion inside the cabin. On another day she might've had a flush of realisation, decided to give privacy where it was due. Perhaps there was some subconscious driving power within her, wanting to warn others away from the follies of falling in love . . . it was everything that countless heartbreak songs claimed it was.

But there was something hypnotic about the cabin.

Something which simply drew her in.

As she approached, her heart beat faster.

There was a slight nip in the air.

She opened the door.

She took in the person set against the gloomy interior.

They froze in their footsteps, as if caught thoroughly red-handed.

"Hello?" Bella tried.

It took her another few seconds to work out just who it was.

And then it struck her.

Perhaps it was the knee-high, white cotton socks.

Or the miniskirt slit an inch up the thigh.

Maybe the lovingly manicured fingernails.

Dorothy.

"Uh, hi, Bella."

Bella glanced about the cabin, immediately feeling herself swept back to those moments she and Robert had shared here. Just thinking about them sent a flush rising in her cheeks. A skittering feeling passed through her veins. Her ribcage contracted, squeezing air out of her lungs. She told herself that she had to hold it together.

"What're you doing here?" Bella asked, her tone coming across far more accusatory than she had anticipated — what was *Bella* doing there?

Dorothy glanced about before meeting her eye. He grinned. "Oh, this and that."

It was then that Bella put the pieces together — that she realised just who the Humble Proprietor had been in the letter.

It was Dorothy.

For some reason, Bella only realised now that Dorothy was wearing a pair of yellow washing-up gloves, and was in the midst of scrubbing away at the tea stains within a pair of mugs. Bella raised a smile of her own. "I love what you've done with the place."

Dorothy flapped away this remark. "It's nothing really. Just something to pass the time." He continued to work at the mugs, held them up to the fading daylight which snuck in through the window, and then laid them down to drain on the sideboard. With a glance at her, he said, "Guess you're not going to be shoving off any time soon, then?" He tutted a couple of times then peeled off his washing-up gloves. "Suppose I'd better put the kettle on."

Once Dorothy had made tea, they sat down at the table, each with their fingers wrapped around their mug. Since Dorothy had become quiet all of a sudden, Bella decided that it must be her turn to pick up the conversation. She thought of the plaque she had seen attached to the outside of the cabin when she had come here with Robert, and found that she couldn't resist. "Who was Swapan Drupada?"

It was as if she had struck Dorothy in the forehead with a particularly heavy rock. He blinked several times, rendered stunned. He stared into his cup of tea, considering something or other, and then he raised his gaze to Bella once more.

"He was everything to me — my *lover*."

An impossibly hot rush of blood pumped around Bella's veins. She knew that she had no right to intrude on this very private aspect of Dorothy's life. Even if Dorothy had made Bella's own love life his business, there was a distinction to be drawn. It was something which was impossible to put a finger on — hard to *really* pin down. Despite everything that had gone on, there was still some sense of optimism about Bella's life, whereas it felt that there was an unbearable sadness weighing on Dorothy's shoulders.

Bella decided to step in. "You don't need to say anything more — just pretend I didn't say anything at all."

Dorothy looked at her with a vacant expression, and she could tell that his mind was elsewhere now. That he was back in what memories of the love they'd shared had to offer him. He was living in a paradise hundreds of thousands of miles away . . . and long gone.

Impossible to recover.

Dorothy met her eye again. "He was the one person who truly understood me — the one person who I could always rely on, always count on. When he . . . when he *went*, it was as if my life ended. As if there was nothing else for me to do on Earth except . . . except wait to join him in . . . in . . ."

But he couldn't summon the fortitude to actually say the word.

Bella understood.

Speaking something aloud only made it real.

Made it a tangible thing.

Bella sipped at her tea and then began to speak, though she made no conscious effort to construct what passed between her lips. "I've seen glimpses of what you're talking about — I think I have a slight idea of what you mean. But I've never experienced it myself; never whole-heartedly."

"I suppose I should be glad that I got to experience it at all, I suppose?"

Bella swallowed hard. "That's one way of looking at it."

"There are those who never experience it in the entire course of their lifetime, your mother . . ." And then, apparently feeling that he had said too much, that he had somehow overstepped the mark, Dorothy drew back.

"No," Bella said, "you're right. I know for a fact that my mother never had the chance to experience it. She never found the right man. Only my father. But . . . who knows? It might not be too late. There might still be . . . *someone* out there for her . . . someone to make her happier than she could ever imagine."

"We can only live and hope."

Bella wondered if she should leave Dorothy alone in the cabin. It was difficult to tell just what he might have wanted, and she couldn't summon the strength to ask him directly. It seemed like it would be such a base, reckless thing for her to do. In the end, though — whether Dorothy wanted her to leave or not — he was the one who asked the next question. "Are things between you and Robert really over with?"

Bella had a mixture of reactions to what Dorothy said. First there was the blunt anger that someone else outside of her own head knew what was happening to Humble . . . and then she recalled how she had told her mother in apparent confidence only for her — as always — to turn around and tell the entire village about it.

Bella never did learn.

Still, seeing that Dorothy knew what was going on, it seemed a waste not to solicit his opinion. She looked him in the eye. "I think so — I don't think I could trust him again."

Dorothy arched an eyebrow. "Just because of some money?"

Again, Bella felt a throbbing fury in her chest. "No, it's not about the money, Humble is far more than that, it's . . ."

"A business?"

Bella's mouth remained open. She still had so much more to say. It was impossible to reduce Humble into a simple, single word like 'business', couldn't Dorothy see that?

And yet she could think of nothing else to say.

She never had been any good in the blazing arguments she had often had with her mother — somehow her mother always managed to say exactly the right thing at the right time, and it seemed that Dorothy possessed the exact same gift.

"This might sound wise, or this might sound wacko," Dorothy went on, "but look at this place we're sitting in." He paused so that Bella could once more take stock of the cabin. "Just *look* at what love built . . . just *look* at the madness that love inflicts, and the scars it leaves, and how it is manifested in the physical world."

"I have to say that when I saw the cabin, the first thing that came to my mind wasn't madness . . . at least not madness derived from love."

"Ah-ha, but that's the thing. Love is shown in all forms — in *any* form — in the form which the person *feeling* the emotion feels fit to express it."

"You think that Humble is . . . an expression of . . . of my *love*?"

Dorothy shrugged. "Maybe."

"But I have no . . . no real tragedies . . . nothing in my past that merits me building some kind of a" — she searched for the word, came across it, thought twice, and then said it anyway — "*mausoleum.*"

"Maybe not in your past. But what about your future?"

"I . . . don't follow . . . how could I build a mausoleum for something that hasn't even happened yet?"

Dorothy sighed then looked across the cabin kitchen, out of the window, into the forest surrounding. He remained like that for a good few moments and Bella thought that — when he spoke again — it would be to change the subject, to cover over what they had said. "You have no idea," he finally said, "what I would give up just so that I might have a few more seconds — just so that *we* could have a few more seconds together . . ."

Another silence hung over them.

Then Bella cottoned onto what he was saying. "You mean," she said, "I should give up something that I've built with my own two hands in the name of love?" She paused for a second, then corrected herself. "In the name of *potential* love?"

Dorothy met her gaze.

Then gave a firm nod.

What exactly was she supposed to do with that?

She drew a sharp breath. "Just one thing," she said. "Why should I bother giving up as much as a toothpick when he doesn't even call?"

30

CRISIS OF CONFIDENCE

*I*n his flat, Robert sat on a window ledge bench which looked out across the sun-dappled London streets. His dangling foot felt warmed by Woss's sleeping body. He could smell the scent of garlic which still clung to his flat from his attempt at cooking up a gourmet Sunday lunch — some ill-fated effort to make himself feel better.

He had succeeded only in making himself feel all the more alone; in this city of nearly ten million people.

After Bella had called him up That Day, he had got so close to calling her back on countless occasions. He had got so far as hearing the *purr* of the connecting tone in his ear. And he had managed to get to three — maybe four — rings. And then he had lost his nerve. Over and over again. He had simply hung up. Three days ago, he had decided that he was not able to do it anymore.

Why bother?

When Robert's phone finally did ring, it nearly shook him clean out of his skin. His first thought when he glanced at the screen was

Bella, but he was quickly disappointed to see that the name which appeared was 'Lord Charles Knightly'. He flirted with the idea of hanging up the call — of putting off this decision for a little while longer — but in the end he answered. He knew that, even with the reputation he had developed over the years, he would be ill-advised to piss off Lord Charles without extremely solid cause. He knew for a fact — from his own personal dealings with the man, as well as the rumours which went about town — that Lord Charles might well forgive, but he certainly did not forget. And he would waste no time sharing just how *unreliable* and *unprofessional* Robert had been throughout their dealings . . . and, to tell the truth, Robert could really have no argument on those accounts.

He *was* unreliable and unprofessional.

No matter how hard he had waged war on those attributes for the entirety of his life.

Lord Charles never phoned anyone personally unless he had very good reason to do so. That wasn't as prima donna as it sounded; Robert knew of many other high-level business executives who would avoid phone calls at all costs, not wanting to get themselves backed into a corner when they didn't have at least a lawyer and a personal adviser on the call with them. Robert sighed then picked up the call.

"Robert?"

"Yes. Lord Charles?

"Have you made up your mind?"

Robert jabbed his fingers into his temple and massaged — suddenly irritated . . . as if a whole hive of angry bees had taken up residence in his skull. "I . . . think so."

"Well, forgive me for sounding picky, but that really doesn't sound definitive." Although there was a spiky edge to Lord Charles's tone at first, it soon softened as he followed it up. "Are you all right Robert? Do you . . . need me to get in touch with someone?"

"No, Lord Charles. No thank you." Robert squeezed his eyes shut, jabbed his fingers deeper into his temple, and then opened his eyes again, seeing that the London skyline had gone all blurry — slipped from focus. "I stand by what I said."

Lord Charles didn't reply right away.

Robert was certain that his personal assistant — George — would be standing to one side; that the two of them would be conspiring nonverbally.

Lord Charles breathed in deeply. "Robert, I really don't want to lose you from this project. What would it take for me to bring you back on board? What would you accept as a show of good faith that I truly value you and require you on my side?"

Robert could hardly believe what he was hearing . . . and yet he *was* hearing it.

Unless he was gravely mistaken, Lord Charles was — metaphorically, at least — down on his knees and begging.

In all his years of dealing with Big City supremos, Robert could hand-on-heart say that he had never been in a remotely similar situation. The only question which lingered on his mind now was what he was going to do . . .

And yet his answer seemed clearer than ever.

Robert squeezed the handset tighter. His toes brushed Woss's fur, and he stirred with a muted growl, before turning over and going back to sleep. "Lord Charles, you asked me to take some time to think about it, and I've had the time to think about it now — my answer is still the same. I cannot continue doing what I've been doing . . . I'm afraid that beyond what might be required for me to pass onto my successor, I see no way forward in this matter."

Although Robert did his best to coat his response with business language, he knew the truth. There was nothing *but* the personal leaking from every word which passed between his lips. He felt his heart beating twice as fast as normal. Every breath he took seemed to scrape the bottoms of his lungs and to summon all the energy of absorbing a punch to the gut.

Lord Charles sighed down the line, and then said, "It saddens me to hear that, Robert, it really does. Thank you for your help, and I wish you all the best for the future."

When Lord Charles hung up, Robert sat for the longest time with the handset pressed against his ear, staring down into the streets — alive with jostling crowds. He knew that he logically should've felt like he was being torn apart from the inside out . . . but he felt . . . *fine* . . . but it was more than that. He felt as if he had done the right thing.

The only thing he was capable of doing.

31

SUNSET SURPRISE

*A*s the summer blazed into life — in full fury — Bella took in the villagers: women in sundresses; men in shorts and shirts, all of them seemingly glowing in the late-morning light.

Bella sat on the doorstep of Molinaar's Cottage — a pleasantly cool glass of freshly squeezed lime juice gently perspiring against her thigh. With nothing much to do except to sit back and absorb Sunday as it played out, she contented herself with taking stock of the varying facial expressions: the contorted grins; childlike giggles; laughter which blasted forth from mouths. Everything about these days seemed to be so unreal, as if it was all happening within the confines of her mind. Maybe she was still back in the city — perhaps she was still in the old familiar office where she had spent the majority of her professional life, scribbling away at some bland material or other, doing her best to bring out that ever-elusive sparkle which would get people to *buy, buy, buy!*

She pinched herself — just to make sure.

Yep, this was really happening.

To be quite honest, Bella was disappointed that it wasn't raining today. It was, after all, the Grand Opening of the Knightly Resort and Leisure Complex.

With that — rather unpleasant — thought on her mind, she helped herself to her feet, using the doorframe to do so. When she had half turned away from the street outside, and had mentally prepared herself to set about doing some much-needed gardening later that afternoon, she heard a familiar voice on her heels.

"Bella?"

Although she knew that she was being ridiculous, she gave herself another pinch.

Still wide-awake.

Or sleeping very deeply.

She turned to look.

It was — as her hearing had promised — Robert.

She expected to see him differently — impossibly changed after all these weeks they'd been apart — but he was just as she remembered. Her heart remembered, too. She felt it throb in her throat. Her stomach dropped several feet.

Robert's long reddish hair hung at his shoulders. Despite the heat, there was no sign of him sweating at all. Unlike the other men in the village, he wore trousers — albeit trousers made of a light-weight material . . . he knew all about how to maintain his image.

How to keep up his sense of style.

"Hi," she said, keeping her tone ice-cold.

Robert took a step towards her, and she realised that Woss wasn't with him.

She was on the point of asking him what he had done with his dog, when Robert took another quick half dozen steps and planted his lips on hers.

Bella's logical response was to raise her hands and to prise his chest away from her own. But there seemed to be a disconnect between her brain and her body. And it wasn't long before any sense of resistance within her had been vanquished. She lost herself within him. All of a sudden, it seemed as if everything else was happening off in the distance — as if the villagers strolling through the streets were nothing more than birdsong or the wind whispering through the trees. She was vaguely aware of the door slamming shut behind them as Robert ushered her back inside. When he got her into the kitchen, he brought his lips up to her ear and asked where Cassandra was — it took almost all of Bella's concentrated effort to respond that she had gone away to see friends for the weekend; that she wouldn't be back for a few days.

She didn't add that there wasn't any reason for Cassandra to live in Molinaar's Cottage any longer seeing as Humble was finished.

Robert was already gently parting her from her clothes.

It seemed so natural to feel her skin beneath his fingers — to feel how she first flinched, and how her skin puckered into goose-flesh as if a freezing-cold draught wafted about the cottage on what was a stiflingly-hot day.

Somehow — *somehow* — Bella dragged her mind back into the present.

She had to exert great effort.

In controlling herself.

In controlling Robert.

But even as she peeled herself away from him, her whole body rigid with anticipation, she found it impossible to sort the thoughts which bounced about her brain like out-of-control ping-pong balls. "I want to know," she said. "I want to know that you're *staying*."

Robert drew back for a moment — that was what she liked about him. He took himself so seriously. He put thought into anything which involved commitment. And that made it all the more important that he had told her that he loved her.

Why would he have told her that if he hadn't first calculated all the possible implications and consequences of the simple phrase?

Their eyes met.

Those honey eyes.

They pinned her to the spot.

"Can we talk later?" Robert said.

And although Bella attempted to speak again, her voice was quashed by the force of their kiss — and soon she gave herself up to all the wonderful sensations flooding through her body.

The sun peeked in around the edges of the curtains. It was afternoon now, Bella knew that much. Sooner or later, they would need to get up. Normal life would have to be resumed.

But it could wait a while longer.

Bella's heart beat low and hard. She felt the blood pumping to her head. Whenever she breathed in, it felt as if her lungs had an impossibly large capacity — as if she might be able to draw in all the air in the world. Robert not only made her feel as if she was someone else, he made her feel as if she possessed supernatural powers . . . as if she could do anything and everything she desired.

Except, she knew, the one thing which she had truly striven for on her own:

Humble Greetings.

She thought about what Dorothy had said — about how she should be glad to sacrifice her business for a chance at experiencing love; that Humble was nothing more than a manifestation of unspent love . . . misdirected love. Just as the cabin was Dorothy's personal mausoleum to his own lost lover . . .

Could it really be true?

She turned on her side, eyeing Robert. "Did you come by to see the Grand Opening?"

Robert held very still for a long few moments, his eyes tracing Bella's. Then he said, "I came by to see you. I don't think that Lord Charles would be best pleased to know that I was so much as in the neighbourhood today."

"Then why *did* you come — today of all days?"

Even though Bella still felt the warmth between them, the easy flow of . . . *love* . . . she felt something throbbing just beneath the surface of her skin. Something which implored her to get the answers she sought.

Robert breathed in, then out.

And Bella almost lost herself in the sensation of his hot, wonderful-smelling exhalation.

"I have a plan," he said.

"A 'plan' for what?"

Robert smiled slightly. There was a devilish sparkle in his eye. "A plan for everything."

3 2

THE GRAND OPENING

*I*t was hard to believe that Bella was actually doing what Robert had suggested she do. She felt almost as if she was a secret agent sent off on some life-threatening mission. It was only Lord Charles's lecherous hold on her forearm which kept her balance — which prevented her from toppling over on the red carpet and making a spectacle of herself.

Bella felt like a different woman entirely. For these hours, she inhabited a completely different body. Her hair was no longer her own — having been replaced by a cropped, black wig Robert had produced from somewhere or other. She had been surprised at how thoroughly the wig had changed her appearance. When she had put on the red dress which Robert had suggested, she hadn't recognised herself in the mirror at all . . . which meant that Lord Charles had stood no chance either.

She still found it almost impossible to grasp just how Robert had managed to talk her into this. But he had said that it was the best plan he could think of to rid Normonswold of Lord Charles for good. And she had been so convinced that there would be no way that the plan would be able to work — that Lord Charles would see straight through such a cheap trick. And yet . . . here she was.

It was just as Robert had planned it.

He had dropped her off at the Thicket Arms Inn — where Lord Charles was staying — and Bella had done nothing other than take a stool at the bar. Not ten minutes had gone by before Lord Charles's personal assistant, George, had somehow spied her and approached, asking her delicately whether she might not mind being Lord Charles's companion for the evening. Bella had agreed to this, in accordance with the plan, and — after having bought her a drink to sip at while waiting — George had brought Lord Charles down from his room. They had left together for the resort in a chauffeur-driven vehicle.

Even though Bella understood logically that there was no reason to feel so, she felt a great sense of having betrayed her mother, and all those of the Normonswold Committee, who had so nobly opposed the Knightly Resort and Leisure Complex. She felt as if she had betrayed herself, too, considering the trick which Lord Charles had played on Humble — making it so that the business would fail. She had to constantly remind herself that these were the last moments she would be required to maintain close proximity with Lord Charles . . . and then it would all be over.

This would be for everyone.

This would be the justice they had all *waited* for.

Flashbulbs went off as Bella walked alongside Lord Charles. She expected Lord Charles to recognise her at any second — to see her for who she was, and to suddenly bring all this to a halt. She had heard that Lord Charles would be employing plains-clothed police officers for the duration of today's event . . . and she couldn't help wondering if she had *really* fooled Lord Charles into making him believe that she was an entirely different girl — that the two of them had never met previously. That he wasn't the one who had crippled her business. That he had found the one *way* of getting to the heart of the opposition to his plans in crushing Humble Greetings like the bug it was; not directly hurting the main perpetrator — Indigo Miles — but instead her daughter. Finding the way to truly stop the protests in their tracks. And to get just what he wanted.

And yet they kept on walking.

Lord Charles had said nothing to her this evening except to greet her and that she 'looked beautiful'. He either had his mind on other things, or women truly were interchangeable beasts to him. No more distinguishable from one another than common garden wrens.

Lights flickered all around, hanging from the trees which surrounded the main resort building. There were several fountains spurting water. Then there was the buzz of conversation coupled with the jazz trio hustling energy through the gathering. Bella found herself on the end of countless wide-mouthed greetings. It seemed as if everyone and anyone wished to meet Lord Charles; the constant stream of people approaching him to pump his hand and say some words of little substance was testament to that. After a while, Bella noticed how a smile clung to Lord Charles's lips. She realised that he was enjoying this thoroughly. That he was *thriving* in this environment as others came up to him and told him how great he was . . . how *wonderful* this resort he had built was . . .

It was then that Bella happened to catch Lord Charles's personal assistant's eye.

George.

The two of them stared one another down, and Bella knew that — if he hadn't already before — George had twigged just who she was. Although she knew that in her role of secret agent this evening she should've broken free of Lord Charles's grip and attacked George before he could reveal her, she administered herself a dose of reality — knowing that there would be no way in the world that she could fight back against the undercover security which no doubt swarmed the Grand Opening.

It happened very quickly. As a garish couple approached Lord Charles — the two of them bearing standard-issue grins — she felt George taking hold of her arm, and of Lord Charles, without protest, allowing George to lead her away.

As each step brought her further and further away from Lord Charles, Bella couldn't help but feel like more and more of an idiot. She had been *stupid* to believe that this plan could work. For a second, she felt a flare of annoyance with Robert . . . he was the one who had been so adamant that everything would work out fine . . . that this would be the *perfect* way to drive Lord Charles from Normonswold for good . . . but now.

It was all too obvious.

It was all too *ridiculous*.

Bella expected George to lead her away from the main crowd, and then for a pack of undercover security men donning tuxedos to take over. She imagined the triumphant expression on George's face as she was led away from the Grand Opening — defeated for the final time.

But no security jumped her.

And — Bella realised — George's hold was loosening.

Then he had let her go completely.

Her greatest urge was to run.

To *get the hell out*.

But she held her ground, perhaps more stunned than anything else.

"It's okay," George said, "I'm in on the plan — I'm in on Robert's plan."

Bella felt confused at what George was saying. She got out the only thing which came into her head. "Why didn't Robert tell me?"

George met her eye briefly before his gaze slipped away, to drift over the gathering at the Grand Opening. "I . . . hadn't made my mind up yet."

"Well, that's . . . reassuring."

His attention locked back onto her. He smiled slightly. "No, it's not what you think. It's not about lack of commitment . . . it's about whether or not this is the right way to do it."

Bella thought of the plan, her attention now slipping across the complex to where Robert had shown her where the septic tanks were buried on the blueprints. That was her destination. She turned back to George. "You had a better plan, then, did you?"

George gave a slight smile, then shook his head. "There can only be one reason why we're actually going through with this, isn't there?"

Bella said nothing. And then she couldn't help but allow the heat in her lungs to pour from her mouth. "Why are you only helping us now? Why didn't you *say* anything before? Why have you been propping up Lord Charles for such a long time?"

George eyed her again, his smile slipping slightly. "You're right," he said. "These are all legitimate questions, but maybe another time?" He drew breath. "The important question is whether or not you believe you can trust me . . . whether or not you're willing to do what I say so that we can successfully execute the plan."

Bella considered for the longest time. And then she decided

that her options weren't exactly great. And why would George even be indulging her in conversation at all if he was truly on Lord Charles's side — wouldn't he just have clicked his fingers and had her thrown from the Grand Opening in a heartbeat . . . or locked up, since she supposed that she was technically trespassing.

She looked back at George. "Okay, I'm in."

George led them through the crowds of well-dressed people — all of them ready to have a Jolly Good Party. As Bella eyed them all, she wondered whether or not they truly knew who the real Lord Charles was. She wondered how many of the women among them had been victim of his unrequited 'charms'.

When they reached the edge of the gathering — the music beginning to drift and quieten on the breeze — George increased their pace. He surely sensed that now they were away from the main group they were more susceptible to detection than ever.

Bella's heart struck at her ribcage. She wanted so much for this evening to be over. She wanted so badly for things to return to normal — to the new normal which she had established over the past few weeks. She wanted to get on with her life.

She wanted to get on with Humble.

She wanted to get on with *Robert* . . .

George brought her close so that he wouldn't need to raise his voice. "You might want to take your shoes."

Indeed, when Bella looked down, she saw that the carpeting which covered the rest of the party space had come to an end. She knew that it would be perilous for the wearer of high heels to set off across the boggy land, but — even so — she still felt a faint reluctance to go wading through muck in her party frock. Hearing the *ting-ting-ting* of a champagne glass being struck by a teaspoon gave her the much-needed push, however.

There was no time to waste.

Bella slipped off the red high heels she had picked out to match her party dress and left them at the edge of the carpet.

George offered her the crook of his arm, and Bella took hold.

She felt his steadying support.

The two of them waded their way through the muck, making their way towards the pair of grim, grey-white monoliths.

With the unmistakable sound of Lord Charles's warbling tones in the background, Bella and George arrived at the septic tanks. It was here that Bella felt a shrill buzz pass through her gut.

Was she really going to do this?

It seemed so.

Was this right? Was this mature?

She thought about how she had once believed her mother to be somewhat childish in the way she had thrown herself into the protests, but now she saw the logic of what she had done — and this was the logical conclusion of everything . . .

"You know what you're doing?" George asked.

Bella felt a buzz of fear. "You're going?"

In the gloom, the intense spotlights holding the landscape back from darkness, she could make out the silhouettes of the party attendees.

"I need to be seen near him when it happens," George replied. "There's no reason for him to suspect me, but — all the same — better not to risk it, eh?"

As George released her from his grip, Bella felt a rush of panic. She wanted to snatch hold of him again, not allow him to go, like some fifties Hollywood heroine. She resisted, though. And perhaps it was only her pride which prevented her doing so.

George smiled at her, then slipped back into the darkness. "When I make the signal — you'll know it when it happens — turn both taps on full . . . okay?"

Bella's throat constricted so tightly that she could no longer summon any sound from her throat. She could only nod.

And George left her alone.

The seconds were longest when Bella was alone once George had re-joined Lord Charles's party. She stood still, feeling a fresh breeze blowing across the Knightly Resort and Leisure Complex. Something within her seemed to be humming. She wasn't certain whether it was encouragement, or if it was fear. She had never felt as alone as she did right now — and she had never felt that she had possessed as much power as she did now.

She could just go home . . .

Pretend she had never even gone out tonight . . .

The only consequence would be Lord Charles wondering where his female companion had got to for the evening — but she didn't imagine it would prove to be any sort of a lingering concern for him. Women, like challenges, were fleeting.

Once he had conquered Normonswold she supposed he would move onto the next.

She approached the septic tanks, her attention partially lingering on the party, wondering just when and how George's signal would come.

To say that Bella had never been this close to septic tanks

before was obvious — just who in their right mind would *want* to get close to a septic tank?

They seemed simple, enough, however.

She saw that the taps jutted out from the back, the spot where the refuse lorries were supposed to set their nozzles and suck away all the nastiness inside.

She breathed in deeply again. She could smell the trees. And the long grasses — growing taller still. And she thought she caught the sharp whiff of a fox. Although she had never been much of a naturist, she couldn't help but wonder about the environmental impact of what Lord Charles was doing; of the impact of what she was about to do now . . . it would all be okay, wouldn't it? It would all be in the name of some higher value?

Some Greater Purpose.

That was all she had now.

She gripped hold of one of the taps.

Waiting.

It would be any moment now.

Why would George waste any more time?

She breathed in deeply.

Her heart struck the underside of her throat rhythmically.

Softly.

It was then that she heard someone approaching.

Her heart stopped beating.

She looked into the gloom, trying to divine just who the person was. Surely it had to be a member of Lord Charles's security detail — their suspicions raised, and coming to investigate the disappearance of Lord Charles's escort for the evening.

She had to act fast.

There was no time for the signal.

She gritted her teeth and channelled all her strength into turning the tap she held . . . and found that it was stuck tight.

The person was getting closer.

Closer and closer.

There was no time!

When the sounds of their approach were loud enough in her ears, she realised that there was no hope of her opening both taps. She would only get away with opening one of them. And for how long? She could only hope that once open, it would be impossible to stop the flow. She felt a firm hand on her shoulder.

And everything stopped dead.

Her strength deserted her.

She had been caught red-handed.

Nothing to be done now.

She had failed.

. . . And yet . . . there was something about the touch — something which sent a tingling sensation through her blood. It swiped right through her, up to her brain, seeming to make her cheeks and temples burn. When her mind caught up with her body, she saw who it was.

Robert.

Confusion reigned for several seconds.

Then she caught up with reality.

He was here.

He was *here*!

And then the danger of it all hit her.

Regaining her strength, she thrust herself upwards, nearly knocking Robert flat on his back. "What're you *doing* here? You're not supposed to be involved in any of this!" She drew a sharp breath — looked out over the party, and to the speech which Lord

Charles was continuing to make. "If Lord Charles finds out . . . what about your career?"

Robert reached out again, and it was only an unchecked sense of delight at seeing him here which kept her from swatting his hand away. He embraced her, bringing her tight against his muscular chest. "I was angling for a bit of a change, anyway. In actual fact, I was wondering about phoning up Humble Greetings on Monday to see if they might be accepting CVs . . ."

Bella was on the brink of telling him that there was no need to phone up, when a bout of laughter brought her back to the present — reminding her just why she was standing in the dark. "Wait," she said, peeling herself away from him. "Was that the signal?"

The two of them stared off across the landscape, to the silhouetted people at the gathering, and to Lord Charles standing on a platform over them — dominating them.

Robert reached down for her hand, tangling her fingers about his. "It was me," he said. "I was the signal."

Bella's whole body went rigid. She looked out to the party, and then back to Robert. She couldn't help herself any longer. She fell into him. Allowed him to squeeze her to his body. They pressed their lips together. She felt his intense warmth . . . a warmth like she had never felt previously — a warmth she had never experienced with anybody else.

It was another bout of laughter that brought Bella back to the present.

Again, she pulled herself from Robert's embrace.

"Okay," she said. "Let's do this."

Robert gave her a firm nod, and they moved to the first tap.

When Robert gave the tap an experimental pair of tugs, he found it was as difficult to shift as Bella had. He stood back, wiping his brow. "You don't reckon the men who come to take this stuff away have some kind of a special tool to get these taps open, do you?"

The very idea that they might have got themselves into this situation only to find no way forward — no way of achieving what they had set out to do — was horrifying for Bella.

"I . . . don't know . . ."

Robert gave the tap another go, and was unsuccessful. He straightened up again. "Maybe if we both try?"

Bella got down beside him. They each took one side of the tap. Bella felt the cold, blunt metal jab into the flesh of her palms. It felt rigid — and yet there was a sense of there being some *give* to the stiff tap . . . if she could only . . .

And then with a joint effort, Bella felt the tap spinning about on its axle.

Once they had got it past the initial stage, it was impossible to stop the tap spinning.

If Robert hadn't reached out and grabbed hold of her forearm she supposed she would've tumbled to the ground . . . and ruined her party frock . . .

"Quickly," Robert said, moving to the other tap.

Despite the sense of urgency, she heard the smile in Robert's voice. She could feel a smile of her own lining her lips. She knew that the two of them delighted in overcoming what had previously seemed to be an unconquerable challenge.

As the stench of sewage began to overwhelm Bella, she helped Robert to loosen the other tap. This time it was much easier. She wasn't sure whether or not the tap was any looser than the other one had been, but it certainly seemed to open much more quickly.

Soon enough, the two of them stood back, the muck pouring forth from the septic tanks, and the stench of it becoming all-consuming.

"Come on!" Robert said, taking her hand, grinning maniacally. "Let's get out of here!"

As they rushed across the soggy earth, making their escape, Bella glanced back over her shoulder. Applause for Lord Charles's speech had broken out. And she watched as a solitary firework spat into the night sky and burst into a thousand glittering pieces.

Soon the celebrations would be over.

Of that there was no doubt.

EPILOGUE

Sitting in the studio at Molinaar's Cottage, Bella felt as if she could take the feeling of pure, unchecked happiness no longer. She closed her eyes and pretended everything had gone away. That she was back in the city, back in her flat, back in the job which she had hated so vociferously . . . the only trouble was that her imagination always failed her before too long. Whenever she thought of the past, a smile would sneak onto her lips. And she would open one eye to see the world as it really was.

Beautiful.

Perfect.

Hers.

She looked down at the greetings cards which she had been working on that morning. They were now each accompanied by their own selection of copy. Although Bella was always the very worst judge, she couldn't help but think that what lay before her on the table represented the very best of her work so far at Humble.

Bella leaned back slightly in her chair, seeing that Woss had — at some point — snuck into the studio and fallen asleep in the corner. He was exhaling deeply and contentedly, and with hardly a sound. She looked at him a long while before deciding to rise up from her work and head for the kitchen. It was almost midmorning — time for another cup of coffee.

When she crossed the threshold into the kitchen, she was surprised to see Robert sitting at one end of the table. He had his laptop out and a cup of coffee of his own smouldering alongside. He looked up when he saw her, his expression serious at first. And then it softened. That always seemed to be the way with Robert. It was almost as if he inhabited another world inside of his mind, only to return to her — *full-heartedly* — at will.

"I didn't hear you getting up," Bella said.

Robert tapped a couple of times at his laptop then rose. "I'm sly like that. Coffee?" Without waiting for her answer, she saw he had already poured her out a fresh cup and left it on the kitchen counter. He handed it over. She took it from him with a smile.

"Thanks," she replied.

Robert leaned against the kitchen counter. Today he was wearing a pair of blue jeans with a loose-fitting chequered shirt over the top. Bella didn't think that she had ever seen Robert look so casual as today. Or as devastatingly handsome. As he sipped at his coffee, he batted his fringe from his eyes.

They drank in silence for a long few moments. There were more and more of those these days. It was a funny thing, back when Bella had been a child, and her parents had been fighting, she had always taken those silences to mean that there was something wrong — that her mother and father were waging a cold war between one flaming argument and the next. That there was tension, and a fresh fight, brewing . . .

There was nothing uneasy about the silence between her and Robert, however.

It was an *easy* silence.

Simply no need for words.

They could communicate without them.

When Robert finally did speak, Bella thought it might be to float the idea of them going out for a walk with Woss, or perhaps for them to take a trip to the shop together. However, the words which came out of his mind had nothing to do with either.

"I used to have these dreams," Robert began. "Just . . . really *weird* dreams."

Bella felt a slight tightness in her chest. She attempted to meet Robert's eye, but he continued to stare down into his coffee.

"I would be walking along this passageway — open windows on either side of me — curtains streaming out through each of them — just this complete blackness everywhere . . . blackness to each side, blackness up ahead . . ."

"What about behind you?"

Robert shook his head. A slight smile tweaked his lips. "I was never able to turn my head, to look behind." He sniffed a laugh and covered his eyes with his hand. "It was just a dream."

Bella allowed the silence to ring out. Then she took her chances. Having finished her coffee, she set her cup down on the side, and then reached her arms about him. He was unresponsive at first, and then he put his own cup down. And she felt him wrap his arms around her. Squeeze her so tightly that she could feel his heartbeat thundering.

They had been standing like that for a while when there was a knock at the door.

Bella restrained the urge to curse. She felt Robert gently peel himself away from her.

"Your mother?" Robert said, with a note of humour.

Although Bella knew it was ridiculous, she felt her face flush. She watched on as Robert made his way to the door. Bella was wondering if it might not be Cassandra — that she had returned from a day out she was spending with friends, or that it might be Dorothy stopping by for a cup of tea and a chat. Robert called for her to come.

As Bella approached the door, something felt off — something which she couldn't quite lay her finger on. She approached Robert's shoulder, wary of using his body as a human shield; of using him to block out all the evils of the world.

Standing there, on the doorstep, was Lord Charles Knightly. As Bella had always seen him previously, he was dressed in a well-turned-out suit. He looked as if he was better prepared for the boardroom than a stroll about Normonswold.

"Good morning," he said, his tone of voice flat, unfeeling.

Bella felt a sharp tingle through her blood. She looked to Robert, seeing that he was similarly rendered stunned by Lord Charles's presence. "What do you want?" Bella found herself asking.

If Lord Charles was offended by the blunt tone of her question, then he offered no clue from his level-headed response. "I thought that by now you would have heard the news."

Bella looked to Robert, who made no motion that he had done.

Lord Charles went on, a slight sigh threatening to choke what he said next. "It will be much to your liking that I have decided to pick up and leave."

Bella said nothing.

In truth, she *felt* nothing.

Everything seemed so distant.

Her role in the opening night for the Knightly Resort and

Leisure Complex had almost been wiped clean from her mind — almost like one of those dreams which Robert had shared with her. These past few days, she had to confess, she had almost entirely forgotten that Lord Charles even existed at all.

"I'm sorry to hear that," Robert said, his insincere reply speaking for both of them.

Lord Charles nodded nonchalantly. Then he looked about the front hall of Molinaar's Cottage, as if he might have been planning on putting up his next resort right there. Finally, though, he turned back to look at Bella and Robert. "I just thought I should tell you that I don't begrudge what you did — what *either* of you did."

Bella knew he was pointedly talking about the septic tanks which had 'spontaneously' burst on the opening night. Maybe Lord Charles had recognised her after all.

"Perhaps," he went on, another sigh in his voice, "I misjudged my plans — my *intentions* for Normonswold . . . it has always been an unhappy habit of mine that I will much rather try and force the arm rather than walk away with grace." He paused. "Well, I am walking away with grace now." There seemed to be something else on his mind — something which was preventing him from turning and going back to his car.

It was then that Bella heard footsteps.

And she saw Lord Charles's personal assistant, George, tread into view.

He bore a gift — wrapped in paper and with a shiny ribbon tied about it.

Without the hint of a smile, he handed it over to Bella.

She took it from him.

Lord Charles nodded to George, and the two of them made to leave. They got into the car and drove away so quickly that both Bella and Robert were rendered speechless.

The two of them stood on the front step, staring out into the road after the departing car for the longest time. It was only when Woss appeared beneath her feet — belatedly arriving to see who had come to call — that Bella regained any sense of reality.

"Should we open it?" she asked.

Robert glanced to her, then looked down at the gift which Bella held. "Okay."

Her heart beat against the underside of her throat as she gently slipped her fingernail beneath the ribbon, dragging it upwards. When the wrapping fell away, she could hardly believe what she was looking at . . . it was a framed picture — a *portrait*. She drew in a deep breath, attempting to keep her shaking hands steady. She saw that it was Molinaar's Cottage in the picture frame — a sketch of the cottage covered in snow. And then, as she looked more closely still, she realised that something was written in the bottom corner of the picture. A hastily scribbled note . . . or an inscription?

My home. I shall never forget. CF.

Bella looked to Robert. "Charles Knightly?"

Robert was rendered stunned. He appeared unable to offer any comment whatsoever. They stared at the picture for several long minutes before turning to go back inside. "I never knew," Robert finally managed to reply. "He must've drawn it when he was younger — a teenager? In his early twenties?"

Bella held the picture another few seconds before handing it over to Robert. She was unsure what to do with it . . . perhaps they would hang it in the hall.

As Bella brought the door shut on Normonswold, feeling Woss brushing past her leg, she reached out for Robert's hand. For his reassuring fingers which gripped her so tightly — with so much love. It felt as if she had come a long way just to come back home.

And she *was* home now.

THE END

AUTHOR'S NOTE

Thank you for taking the time to read one of my books. If you would like to hear about my latest releases you can sign up for my newsletter here: www.essiepowers.com

Thanks for reading!

Essie Powers

Humble Greetings
The First Humble Greetings Novel